Damaged Billionaire's Surprise Heir

Gwynne Hart

Contents

CHAPTER 1

Sydney

"She's not here, is she?"

My office manager, Jane, hesitates, not wanting to confirm what I already know. "No, she isn't. But I can—"

"I've had enough of Sara's recent erratic behavior! We've been working hard on the therapy plan for this new client, and I cut her some slack for the extra hours. But I've had enough of her tardiness and excuses."

"Sara *is* PTX's top therapist and—"

"And we landed this client because PTX is known for our success with tough sports rehab cases. I refuse to let her tarnish our reputation... *my* reputation." I let out a sharp breath, sinking back into the plush leather chair. "Enough with the excuses. When is the client expected to arrive?"

Jane's brows furrow. "The client will be here soon, but they didn't specify a time for 'security' purposes," she says.

My mind churns furiously.

My clinic, PTX Sports Therapy, has worked with many celebrity clients, but I have been told that this client is more than your average bench-warming NHL player or star college athlete. The family is conservative and secretive. They have made a substantial deposit for the initial design of the treatment regimen.

PTX offers specialized services. We look successful but we're struggling financially within our narrow focus. I want to expand PTX, diversify services, to secure its future. A successful rehabilitation for this client will go a long way to making the expansion a reality. We can't afford to lose whoever this client is. Although we designed the treatment plan together, Sara is the therapist named and assigned to handle this client's physical therapy.

Revealing Sara's absence would undoubtedly pose problems. However, the client has never seen her before. All they know is the name of the qualified therapist— "Sara Jensen."

I firmly press my lips together, contemplating a plan. It carries significant risks that could backfire, but it will secure my company's future if everything works out. Since they want Sara Jensen, I will give them Sara Jensen.

In the silence, Jane is visibly anxious. I am agitated also but I suppress it. Being the leader, I have to appear confident. "When they arrive, I want you to inform them that the owner is unavailable, but Sara is ready to meet with them," I say.

Jane stares at me, eyes wide with surprise. If I was in her place, I suppose I might react similarly. "But Sara isn't..."

"I will pose as Sara until this job is completed."

"B–but isn't that... are you sure that's not illegal?"

"It's a fine line. But they've hired PTX. Not Sara. And I'm more experienced than Sara. We can sort out any complications later. We must secure this contract." I suddenly feel the full burden of business ownership on my shoulders. This is not going to be easy.

"In the meantime, Jane, keep trying to contact Sara. Call her emergency contacts. And the local hospitals."

Still staring at me as if I've grown two heads, Jane backs out of the room. She retreats to the front desk while I remain in my empty office, trying to wrap my head around the possible repercussions of my decision and the imminent turbulence ahead. It is a daring plan full of risks, but if it works, it will be the best course of action to maintain our image and plans.

As I wait, the ticking of the clock fills my office, intensifying the gravity of my decision. Time drags on, heightening my unease with each passing moment. Doubt creeps in, whispering the risks of my actions. What if the client suspects a problem? What if my true identity comes to light? Yes, I'm risking ethical and licensing problems, but I also know this client is extremely impatient for results. Results I'm sure we can deliver.

I push those thoughts aside, reminding myself of the stakes involved. This client is the key to saving *and* expanding my business, as well as securing a promising future for my son. Being a single parent, I'm all he has.

Minutes turn into what feels like hours. Finally, there is a discreet knock on my office door. I inhale deeply, an attempt to prepare myself for what lies ahead. "Come in." Squaring my shoulders, I try to project a confidence I don't feel.

"Mrs. Romero, they have arrived," Jane says as she sticks her head in the door.

"It is Ms. Pearce, Jane. Sydney Pearce, not Sydney Pearce Romero. We've gone over this already," I correct her gently, rising from the comfort of my leather seat. I am no longer married, so the title—Mrs.—is no longer appropriate, and neither is Romero.

"Or better yet, Miss Jensen. It's best to get used to the name," I say, reaching for the files on my desk originally intended for Sara. The bundle of paperwork will prove essential to my newly assumed role.

"Miss Jensen, they have arrived," Jane echoes, stepping aside and allowing me to walk out my office door.

"Good practice, Jane." A mild chuckle escapes me unintentionally, calming the nerves built up in anticipation.

"Just playing my part," Jane quips as she leads the way to the waiting clients.

We walk towards our board room, and I catch sight of a group of men in suits sitting around our oval table, talking among themselves. The room has partially frosted glass for walls, and they seem clueless to my proximity as they converse intently. The closer I get, the more I feel the violent thumping of my heart in my chest.

Jane crosses the threshold into the meeting room in front of me to lead the introductions. "Gentlemen, Miss Jensen," she says as she gestures in my direction.

Rolling chairs screech around the room as the men stand to greet me. "Pleased to meet you, Miss Jensen," the oldest-looking man among them says, extending a hand to meet mine. I reach out, giving a firm handshake. He then gestures to the door. "Shall we?"

The original plan was to meet here at PTX, but I received a call early this morning informing me of a sudden venue change. We are to meet the client at his estate.

"Of course. Please lead the way," I quickly oblige, noticing the urgency emitting from the group.

Jane, whose presence I had momentarily forgotten, cut in. "I'll lead you to your vehicles."

"Mr...?" I ask, wanting to address him directly.

"Cecil Holmes. I am the official handler of my client's medicals," he explains, his monotonous tone somewhat off-putting.

"You compiled the treatment records?"

"Correct. Three years of records."

I hoped to engage him in conversation, but his aloof demeanor makes it clear that he is uninterested in small talk.

Silently, we follow Jane as she maneuvers through PTX's brightly lit halls to the back entrance of the building. The fast clacking of thick soles echoes through the small space before being drowned out by the noise of running motors outside. Three sleek, black cars with black-tinted windows await us just outside the door.

"Miss Jensen," Cecil's flat tone calls out as a young, well-built man pulls open the back door of a black car, lined up among two others.

"Thank you," I politely offer my gratitude, carefully stepping into the vehicle, settling into its seat, and placing the files on my lap. Cecil enters after me but maintains a considerable distance.

A man of few words, Cecil does not engage me in any type of conversation while the car glides through San Diego's bustling streets. The passing scenery visible through the tinted windows is the only thing available to occupy my mind.

My thoughts grow louder and louder in my head as the silence in the car continues. I start to question the soundness of my idea. Deep down, I know my uneasiness is rooted in desperation. PTX may appear well off from the outside, but only I am truly aware of the financial turmoil within. I need this to work out.

Before long, we arrive at an airfield. The situation becomes more tense as I catch sight of a helicopter, its blades spinning wildly against the wind. Cecil and his escorts swiftly exit the cars, guiding me toward the helicopter. As we get closer, the noise increases, reverberating through the air.

Reality is starting to sink in. Here I am, having assumed someone else's identity, flying to meet a reclusive client who holds the future of my rehabilitation center in his hands. It feels as though the helicopter's noise and wind are trying to knock me back, but I push forward alongside Cecil, who offers me a hand to climb into the cabin and take my seat.

What are the odds of everything aligning? Of this crazy plan working?

Cecil grabs my attention as we take off. "We're headed to the Hartwell estate," he yells over the deafening roar of the chopper.

My heart drops for a moment, leaving me briefly breathless. "I'm sorry, what?" I shriek, anxious, hoping I had misheard what he said with all the noise.

"What?" he yells.

"Where are we going?" I yell back.

"Yes, we'll be there soon." Cecil yells.

I shake my head. I'm sure I must have heard him wrong. I only know one Hartwell, and I don't think it's him. Although two out of three facts match—hockey player; car accident. The three years of intense therapy—that timeline doesn't match up. Besides, I don't believe he's in the San Diego area. He doesn't have an estate nearby. Another hockey playing relative? Odd coincidence.

I glance down at the sprawling city. Green and concrete stretch for miles, specks moving about, disappearing out of sight the farther we travel. My son is in one of those buildings with my ex-husband. My son, Damon, would relish the excitement of flying over the city in a helicopter. Thinking of his joy helps me forget some of the nerves gnawing at me.

Eventually, the estate comes into view. Vast stretches of grassland surround an oversized, opulent mansion at the center. The word "mansion" seems inadequate to capture its true magnitude. There are a few smaller buildings in the surrounding areas, one I recognize as a stable.

As we descend, I see a group of people and more black vehicles near the mansion. Judging by the helicopter's trajectory, we are heading toward them. Although I can't yet see his face, I am certain the man with the cane is my client.

I tightly grip a random iron bar inside the helicopter while clutching the files tightly with my other hand, bracing myself for the landing. The aircraft slowly descends before touching the ground, its blades still spinning at full speed. Cecil and I disembark, hastily distancing ourselves. Once it takes off again, I pat down the loose strands of my hair and adjust my blazer.

Satisfied with my appearance, I focus on the crowd ahead, scanning them in search of the man I had seen with the cane.

As my eyes focus on him, my breath hitches and stalls as I fight to keep breathing. An unsettling chill permeates my body, leaving me feeling frozen in place with my eyes fixated on him.

Gabriel.

It's him. He who supposedly did not return to San Diego. *The* Gabriel Hartwell, is standing mere feet from me. He's right here, only steps away. It's clear from his expression that he doesn't recognize me or remember our history. If only I could do the same.

Fate is beyond cruel. It's been a decade since I last saw him. Ten long years since he left me to endure one of the most challenging times of my life. Ten long years since I last held him in my arms.

"Miss Jensen?" A heavy touch on my shoulder awakens me from my daze, and I breathe in the warmth from the surrounding air, willing my lungs to begin working again. "Are you alright?" Cecil asks as I turn to face him.

I nod. "Shall we?" And gesture for him to lead the way.

Gabe's smoldering eyes rake me over appreciatively, then remain fixed on me, intense and unyielding. I'd avert my gaze if I had the strength to do so. With each crunching step on the gravel, I inch closer to him. *He looks so good!* I have the urge to reach out to him, hold him, but I shouldn't. I can't. I am not who they expect me to be. But I am not Sara Jensen—I am Sydney Pearce, former fiancée of Gabriel Hartwell.

"Good day, Mr. Hartwell," Cecil says, his tone now infused with an enthusiasm that had been notably absent during our brief exchanges.

"Good day." Gabe nods, his chestnut brown hair glistening in the sunlight. I use the momentary distraction to take in his muscular yet elegant composure as he leans slightly on the slender ivory stick clutched in his right palm. I melt inside as I picture his defined abs, muscular upper body and firm hockey butt.

After briefly focusing on Cecil, his striking emerald green eyes turn back to me, and his roving gaze turns questioning. "Have we met before, Miss Jensen?" he asks. "You look familiar."

My words catch in my throat, and memories tear at my mind. *We have*, I long to say. We have met in places and ways that words alone could never capture. I want to scream it from the rooftops, but it doesn't matter what I say or how I say it. Gabriel Hartwell will not remember me or the love we once shared.

Tragically, he had lost his memory.

CHAPTER 2

Sydney

I can still feel the remnants of fear that surged through my body upon hearing of Gabe's accident on the news ten years ago. The accident that cut short his NHL career after one record-breaking rookie season and claimed the lives of his older brother and sister-in-law.

Months of agonizing silence followed as I anxiously awaited updates on his condition from his family, but no one ever reached out to me. I was not surprised. The Hartwells had never truly acknowledged the seriousness of our relationship. I was simply a sprinter on a full-ride scholarship at the same university as Gabe, with a fleeting infatuation for him that was undeserving of their social status.

Initially, it had hurt me that he never attempted to seek me out, but then I discovered the painful truth about his amnesia from Brad, Gabe's best friend at the time. Gabe had lost all fragments of himself because of the accident, memories and all. He didn't even know I existed, and his family surely wouldn't remind him.

Brad had told me Gabe recovered in Los Angeles and never returned to San Diego. All my efforts to locate him had proved futile. I eventually gave up. Yet, here he is, standing right in front of me. It's unreal.

I search his eyes, seeking any flicker of true recognition. They remain empty of the once-vibrant spark that characterized our relationship. His eyes hold nothing but curiosity. It's probably for the best, as I am not here as Sydney Pearce, his ex-fiancée, but as Sara Jensen, his physical therapist.

I clench my fist, tightening its grip on the files as I muster a smile. "No, Mr. Hartwell. You must be mistaking me for someone else."

His furrowed brows ease, and a trace of disappointment flickers across his face as if he had been hoping for something more. "My apologies. It seems my memories are playing tricks on me. And please, call me Gabe."

"It is perfectly all right." I spin to face Cecil, unable to bear looking at him any longer. "How should we proceed?"

"Hugh here will provide you with a tour of the mansion and ensure a smooth arrangement for your accommodations," Gabe interjects sharply, pointing toward one of the men beside him as he shifts slightly on his cane.

After he speaks, a realization dawns on me. "Accommodations?" My surprise is hard to disguise. Our priority was to discuss his exercise regimen and therapy, while accommodations were to be addressed later. What prompted the change?

"Yes, you will move into the estate today. Do you have someone who can assist with transporting your luggage?" he casually inquires, leaving no room to question his previous statement.

"I do, but we agreed to—" I attempt to interject.

"Good. Hugh will take charge from here," he says, cutting me off and shifting as he turns away, using his broad back to signal the end of any further discussion. The nerve of him! When did he become so pushy and authoritative?

I watch as Gabe gets into one of the sleek cars, and they drive off to the mansion. The absurdity and high stakes of the situation weigh on me like a ton of bricks.

Cecil turns to leave. "Mr. Holmes, I have some questions before you go.'

He pauses and turns back. "Mr Holmes, when was Mr. Hartwell's accident?"

"Ten years ago," says Cecil.

"Why were only three years of rehab records sent to us? We asked for all records."

"That's all we had. Mr. Hartwell stayed in a convalescent home just outside of L.A. for a year. He had rehabilitation therapy continue through the next 5-6 years but it wasn't intensive."

"What happened during those 5-6 years? He wasn't playing hockey..."

"He completed the business studies he abandoned when he was drafted by the NHL. Then he started working at Hartwell Enterprises. Moved to this estate, taking it over. It was to be his brother Blake's estate but Blake died in the accident. And he moved to sled hockey. Then 3 years ago, he decided he wanted another shot at the NHL. But the pain in his leg, mainly his left knee, is the only thing holding him back. It's incredible how he's regained his skills."

"His skills? Stamina, stick handling... Mr. Holmes, how can he regain those skills if he can't skate?"

"Sled hockey. He's got terrific game sense. His slapshot would be deadly if he could just stay upright. Intense therapy for his legs only started 3 years ago. So that's what we sent you. Just his leg treatment records."

"Just his legs? He's not competed in the NHL for 10 years. Sled hockey and the NHL. All they have in common is the word hockey."

"I disagree, Miss Jensen. His upper body strength from sled hockey makes him stronger than he was in his rookie NHL year. His core is definitely stronger. His game sense and strategy on the ice were what set him apart from any rookie. His amnesia hasn't robbed him of that skill. He had never played sled hockey before. Nobody believes how nimble he is in the sled. It's like he's grafted to the sled. He's determined to succeed."

"I see."

"Miss Jensen, we contacted PTX because of your breakthroughs with athletes who came to PTX having exhausted all other therapies. Do for Mr. Hartwell what you've done for others. Mr. Hartwell will get his stickhandling back if you fix his knees. Now, please, Hugh is waiting for you, Miss Jensen."

I turn toward Hugh. The tall, older man stands gracefully in his distinguished butler's attire. Despite his curly gray hair, there are hardly any wrinkles on his aged face. He appears to be amiable enough, with just a slight upward curve of his lips and a mild gaze. I approach him, the sound of crunching gravel underfoot punctuating the silence as I walk. Hugh nods and motions for me to follow him to the sole remaining car left behind by Gabe's entourage.

The silver lining in this unusual situation is that I, or rather Sara, have the responsibility of helping Gabe recover from his leg injury. If I succeed in my role, it will ensure PTX's expansion. However, I am struggling to adjust to the surprise responsibility of being my amnesiac ex-fiancé's physical therapist. To complicate matters, I am now expected to live on the estate with him.

I carefully place the files on the cream leather seat of the car, relieved to free my hands from the weight of the paperwork. I slide my hand into the inner pocket of my blazer to retrieve my phone. I quickly swipe across the screen and locate Jane's contact information.

I rapidly tap the screen and send her instructions for preparing and transporting my luggage, and re-arranging my appointments. Jane will re-arrange schedules for Robyn and Nicole, the two top PTs after Sara, and schedule them to take my bookings. Jane updates me that Sara's emergency contacts do not know where she is either, and she has not been admitted to any local area hospitals.

Another name catches my eye: Brad Romero, my ex-husband. Considering the sudden turn of events and my revised schedule, it will be better to call him instead of texting him. Our son, Damon, will have to stay with him a while longer. Brad will be very surprised to hear Gabe is my client.

With my phone back in my pocket, I focus on the looming Hartwell mansion as we drive past a fountain. The car halts at the entrance. Hugh, seated next to the driver, is the first to get out and open my door.

I step out of the car onto the gray cobblestone driveway, struck by the grandeur of the entrance. Double doors of ebony tower before me, with wrought iron, intricate carvings, and polished brass fixtures. The entrance is magnificent. Grand white marble columns support the black gable roof with neatly trimmed shrubs on either side.

Hugh easily opens the heavy doors, suggesting his frequent use. As soon as I enter, the elegant marble walls, perfectly matched wrought iron staircase rails, and onyx doors capture my attention.

"Please." The elderly man's raspy voice echoes through the space. "This way."

I follow Hugh, our shoes clicking against the polished floor as he describes each passing room. The echoes of my footsteps seem to stretch on endlessly. Rounding a corner, we see a young girl sitting on the marble floor. She is so engrossed in her books that she doesn't even notice us.

"Miss Katie!" Hugh quickly approaches the little girl. "You should be reading in your room." His tone holds a tinge of reprimand, yet the gentle manner in which he raises her up reveals his fondness for the child.

Katie looks about Damon's age but is quite petite. Her dark curly hair hangs in two symmetric pigtails tied with ribbons. She looks delicate with her slight frame, dressed in a pink floral print dress and white tights, but her missing shoes hint at a more adventurous side.

"I'm bored. Dad left me here when he went to pick up his leg doctor." Katie scrunches her brows, and her lips curl up in defiance. She is quite endearing with her expressiveness.

I'm trying to piece it together, but Hugh confirms my fear as he introduces her. "Miss Jensen, this is Katie Hartwell, Mr. Gabriel's daughter." He gestures toward the pouting girl at his side and continues, "Katie, say hi to Miss Jensen, your dad's... your dad's leg doctor," coughing lightly.

It hits me—of course, he has a family of his own. I'm going to be living in the same mansion with Gabe, his daughter, and whoever his wife might be. A sharp pain tugs at my chest.

Katie glances at me, her blue eyes revealing her curiosity. "Hi," she utters, her voice barely above a whisper.

"Hello, Katie." I attempt to match her mellow tone despite my unease. How will this arrangement affect her, being thrust into a new dynamic with a stranger taking care of her father, living with them? How will his wife feel?

Hugh gently reminds her to go back to her bedroom and continue her reading. She complies reluctantly, casting one last curious glance in my direction before scampering off. As she disappears down the corridor, I can't help but wonder, in another life, if she could have been my daughter... with Gabe.

The tour ends at my assigned room. As soon as Hugh leaves, I let my body sink into the luscious pillowy mattress, surrendering to its luxurious comfort. A sense of anticipation looms before me, but weariness has taken its toll, leaving me unable to contemplate the challenges ahead, the waves of exhaustion from even thinking about Gabe pulling me under. The room gradually dissolves into a soft haze as I let out a breath. And then, before I know it, I'm out like a light.

I greet Jane outside as she arrives with my luggage. I can see the excitement bubbling up inside her when she sees the magnificent mansion and the exquisite elegance of my room.

"The Hartwells are one of the elite families in San Diego," she gushes. "I remember Gabriel Hartwell was quite the rebel, and a tabloid favorite. He's gorgeous."

"He wasn't that wild, Jane. He was the younger son. His brother, Blake, was the Hartwell heir, so they let Gabriel chase his hockey dreams and drop out of university when he was drafted by the NHL. Hockey... unusual for a California boy."

"You seem to know a lot about him."

"Mm... Like you said, he was in the news."

Once I'm able to shoo Jane out the door, I call my ex-husband to inform him of the situation. Brad is surprised to hear Gabe is my client. He had also lost touch with Gabe after the accident.

Brad tells me Damon is still at school, so I don't get to talk to him today. He is thrilled to have more time with Damon. Although Damon might be surprised by the sudden change in plans, I think he will enjoy his extra time with my ex-husband.

Today, I will discuss the therapy plan Sara and I put together with Gabe and hopefully complete our first session. We think his recent setbacks and lack of progress are due to over-training, compounded by choosing inappropriate exercises. Sara has specifically recommended swimming for Gabe because of its low-impact nature, which will be beneficial for his joints and help improve the endurance and mobility of his legs before adding weight-bearing activities. As a certified and experienced physical therapist, I understand the logic and validity behind the suggestion.

But because of our past history, I dread the awkwardness of seeing Gabe almost naked in the pool. Although ten years have passed, vivid memories of us have me wet and wanting. And the thought of him having a family, a wife, hurts so deeply it's difficult to bear. Hopefully, I'll be able to keep my heart out of it and remain professional during our sessions.

As I wait for Gabe to arrive, I inhale deeply, reminding myself to focus solely on his rehabilitation. I *will* maintain a professional demeanor as Sara Jensen. It is easier said than done. I just have to do it.

The warm air in the well-lit pool area holds the pungent scent of chlorine. The sound of rippling water against the blue-tiled floor immediately provides a relaxing atmosphere, calming my nerves.

"Sara, I apologize for keeping you waiting." Gabe's deep voice breaks through the ambiance, interrupting my thoughts. I turn toward him, plastering a smile on my face, and attempting to push the ache in my chest aside momentarily.

"No need to apologize, Gabe." I focus on keeping a steady tone for my speech. "I understand that you have a busy schedule."

With a nod, he gestures toward the pool, his hooded gaze briefly lingering on me before turning away. "Shall we begin?"

We stride toward the edge of the pool, our feet slipping slightly on the wet concrete. The shimmering blue water and the overhead lights create a serene atmosphere despite the tension in the air.

"I don't mean to be rude, but as a hockey player, is swimming the best thing for my legs?" His eyes question me as he places himself in the water. "I am sure you know. This isn't a sports injury."

"I'm aware." I am painfully aware of the cause of his injury. The accident caused far more than just physical harm. "I understand your concern. But in your case, swimming offers several advantages."

"I've tried just about everything else."

"I'm surprised swimming hasn't been suggested before now. Your recovery might have been complete by now."

"I know it's been a while. I thought sled hockey could fill the gap but it's not the same, not fast enough. The wholeness I get from skating, playing hockey... not a memory, a feeling. And now, I've got maybe a year before it no longer makes sense to get back into pro hockey."

"Since swimming is a low-impact exercise, it won't put excessive strain on the joints affected by your accident, allowing for gentle and faster rehabilitation." I enter the pool, the water enveloping my body. "And the buoyancy of water can help support your body weight and promote improved mobility for your legs."

He hums in response as he swims closer to me. His proximity catches me off guard and sends a wave of unease through me. What should I do now?

CHAPTER 3

Gabriel

It is perplexing.

As I float in the pool, the warm, soothing water enveloping my body, I feel like I have met Sara Jensen before, but her identity remains just out of reach. Her smile seems to mock me with its familiarity. And it isn't only that. I feel a tug toward her, an attraction pulling me like the pool is suddenly an ocean, and the waves are insistent. My fingers twitch with the need to touch her, and I clear my throat.

I swim toward her. The nagging feeling of déjà vu is growing, but specifics remain hazy and indistinct. Sara insists that we are merely getting acquainted for the first time. Surely, there is no reason for her to deny any past connection. Unless, I wonder, had I unwittingly caused her pain? Perhaps I knew her before the accident. I push aside the unsettling thought.

Her hazel eyes widen as I approach, and I notice her gulp nervously. Maybe the situation is uncomfortable for her–swimming alone with a stranger, particularly a man, in unfamiliar territory. This would undoubtedly fluster any woman, no matter how professional the circumstances. I contemplate taking charge of the conversation, guiding it to reduce her unease. No. I feel no obligation to make things easier for her. Sooner or later, Sara will have to acclimate to our situation–I need it to be sooner. The faster my recovery, the faster I can return to the ice.

I've played it safe for far too long. I recall with unwavering confidence that hockey remains the only aspect of my identity. I still dream of it–the sensations of gliding across the ice, charging at opponents, slapping the puck, and the feeling of victory. But dreams alone do not suffice.

I've attempted to recapture those sensations, yearning to relive the glory of my dream. Yet, each time I get close to achieving my goals, my knees, damaged by the accident, betray me, bringing my entire body down. As much as I hate to admit it, my mental health is also suffering greatly. I think that's why my mother became so insistent about this therapy arrangement.

I need to feel it again, to taste the exhilarating rush of playing hockey. This is the only thing I hope to salvage from the accident, if nothing else.

"I've seen so many therapists. Your program might be my very last resort, Sara."

She pauses for a moment, her gaze holding mine.

"I'm sure you understand my expectations for this therapy."

Sara responds with a gentle nod. "Can you float on your back, Gabe?" Her fingers gingerly graze the skin of my arm, leaving goosebumps in their wake.

Quietly, I oblige, allowing my weight to shift as I fall back into the water. Her left palm rests lightly on my chest, barely making contact, while her right hand gently lingers at the edge of my back. I find myself hyper-aware of every point of contact she makes.

"Flutter kicks... Let's see how you manage with them. To the end and back." Her eyes briefly dart toward my legs, where the scars are visible. I brush aside the reactive anger, briefly invading my thoughts. I'm sure she means no harm by her quick glance. She is a medical professional, merely assessing my injury.

My muscles begin to burn with exertion as I lift and lower my legs, each motion propelling me through the water. I sustain the rhythmic pattern for a while. Occasionally, I take a moment of respite, easing the tension in my muscles.

A dull throb starts in my leg, and within moments, it escalates into a sharp pain. It seems to materialize out of nowhere, growing into unbearable pain. Staggered by the pain, my breathing seizes, immobilizing me. I abruptly halt my legs' rhythmic pattern in the water and try to take some deep breaths. I need a moment to collect myself. Still on my back, I propel myself back to her with mostly my arms.

"Are you—" she starts but catches herself. "Can you describe the pain, Gabe?" Her eyes squint, like she somehow feels my pain, as she shifts her attention to my legs.

It seems like every day brings with it a fresh reminder of my fragility and limitations, and my patience is wearing thin. I desperately want to take charge of the situation, to resist being at the mercy of my injury.

"Enough for today. That's all I can handle," I say harshly as I quickly upright myself and head for the steps.Surprised by the sudden end of our first therapy session, Sara cocks her head to one side and looks at me. Her eyebrows furrow like she's considering arguing with me, but then she eases up and nods. "Of course. We can continue tomorrow."

I acknowledge her with a curt nod and swim toward the pool's edge, feeling a sense of urgency to put some distance between us. The ache persists, throbbing with each step I take.

I leave the pool area stiffly and limp to the sanctuary of my bedroom. The marble floor is unyielding, causing me to wince with each painful step. As I approach my room, a flicker of movement catches my eye. I turn. At the end of the hallway, I get a glimpse of Hugh's tall figure. His hands carefully balance a teetering stack of books as he navigates the path to Katie's bedroom.

"Hugh!"

He halts and turns. "Sir? Why are you back so early from your session?" He frowns, his wrinkles emphasized as his brows furrow.

An honest revelation of the truth would trigger a barrage of criticism, so I keep it to myself. A part of our family, Hugh meddles in my affairs even when I wish he wouldn't.

"Where is Katie?" I shift the conversation.

Hugh clears his throat. "She's been waiting for you in your study, sir. She seems eager to show you something she has been working on."

I grunt in acknowledgment. Katie has always had a creative spark, a trait that seems to diverge from the Hartwell family's athletic tendencies. She must have gotten it from her mother. I wonder what she has in store for me this time. "Please let her know that I'll be there soon."

I excuse myself and make my way to my bedroom, going straight to the bathroom. The aborted session still lingers in my mind, but I need to freshen up before meeting my daughter. I impatiently shed the damp, black spandex clinging to my skin before stepping into the glass-walled shower space. With a swift twist of the bronze faucet, scalding water rushes over my weary body, washing away the remnants of my swimming session. As steam slowly fills the bathroom, my mind wanders straight back to Sara Jensen.

She was quick to conceal her emotions about how our session ended. Perhaps it was hasty of me to end it so abruptly. I instinctively reach for the broad scar beneath my right knee, delicately tracing the faded skin. Her gaze unsettled me, and I didn't appreciate her staring.

With a heavy sigh, I turn off the water and step out of the shower. As I wrap myself in a plush towel, my mind drifts back to Sara–specifically, her curves, undisguised by her conservative swimwear. With a groan, I force the tantalizing vision from my mind.

I hobble to my closet, grab a clean T-shirt and a pair of sweatpants, and dress quickly. I'm sure Hugh will disapprove of my casualness and give me a frown. I grin to myself. I hurry to my study, where Katie is waiting for me. As I near, I hear her piping voice and smile. Clutching the ebony handle, I pull the door open.

Katie has settled comfortably into one of the leather chairs at my desk, absorbed in a book. She is the spitting image of her mother, Ella, with her gentle features and blue doe eyes, though her dark hair clearly came from my brother. My amnesia makes it impossible to remember either of them, but I have the photographs, allowing me to compare their features to those of Katie.

I swallow the lump in my throat and call out, "Katie."

Katie lifts her attention from the book, a radiant smile illuminating her youthful face. "Daddy!" She releases the book and springs to her feet. She hurries toward me, crashing into my legs and wrapping her arms around them.

I suppress a wince and smile. "Hey, princess." I crouch down to lift her. "I heard you have something special for me."

Excited, her hair lightly bounces as she nods and describes her latest drawing, one of me wearing a crown. Her imagination is a constant source of wonder. I hold the drawing close. I can see the fine details in her art and feel her passion. Sadness and guilt sweep through me as I gaze at the sketch. Despite my best efforts, I can't shake the feeling that I am not worthy of being her father. I feel detached from the drawing. My brother, her biological father, would hold it closer to his heart.

But the accident had taken him away from her. He died, and I was left to live.

The weight of injustice is almost too much to bear. It was a tragic loss for her to have both parents taken from her at such a tender age. She was under a year old and can't recall much about them. I suppose that makes two of us.

Providing her with a nurturing and caring presence has been a challenge, especially when I am struggling with my own uncertainties. My own doubts and insecurities need to be resolved before I can become a positive influence in her life.

First, I need to address my injured leg before doing anything else. The one person who can help me now is Sara Jensen. The image of her hips flashes through my thoughts. My heart skips a beat, and I grimace inwardly. Such thoughts are disrespectful. She is a professional dedicated to helping me fully recover. I have to stay disciplined and stop wandering into inappropriate territory.

Gently folding Katie's drawing, I tuck it into the inner pocket of my jacket. "I'm hiding this so Grandma won't try to take it again." My mother obsessively collects Katie's drawings.

Her laughter fills the room, raising my spirits. "You can keep it. It's yours!" The joy of her words echoes around the room.

"That didn't stop her last time!" I huff as she bursts out into another round of laughter. Although I cannot replace her parents, I have vowed to do my best to make up for their absence and ensure her happiness.

CHAPTER 4

Sydney

I have reached my breaking point.

Gabe's aversion to rehab is obvious. He hasn't shown up for his session for the third time this week. I tap my foot impatiently, waiting for the sound of his footsteps coming down the hallway to break the silence.

Despite my many attempts, our schedules never seem to align. Hugh's advice to avoid his study leaves me with limited options.

Our last session ended abruptly, and I worried I had offended him. I've replayed the session in my head for the past four days. I had been professional and composed, avoiding physical contact as much as possible.

What went wrong?

A frustrated huff escapes me, followed by an audible groan as my irritation grows. I can no longer afford to be passive in this situation. If I don't take action, all my efforts will be for naught, and PTX will suffer. Not only will this hurt my company's reputation, but I could also lose the opportunity for the expansion.

To secure funding for PTX's expansion, we departed from our usual public program setup and agreed to a series of private sessions with this client. Not realizing the Hartwells were the client, I said yes without hesitation. I couldn't afford to let the opportunity pass us by.

I make my way to the main house, scanning for Hugh. Chief of staff and always willing to help despite his crusty demeanor, Hugh surprised me when he delivered dinner to me on my first night at the mansion. Now, I'm hoping he might have information about Gabe's whereabouts.

"Hugh, do you know where Gabe is? He missed another session today."

Hugh's brow furrows, creating deep lines on his forehead. "I saw him heading toward his bedroom," he says. "Perhaps you should check there."

Annoyed, I thank Hugh and hurry with purpose to Gabe's bedroom. I attempt to unclench my jaw as I knock lightly on the door. I hear chair legs scrape against the floor inside, but Gabe isn't responding. In my frustration, I open the door and barge right in.

I shouldn't have done that. The sight before me knocks the breath right out of me, and I feel heat flood my cheeks. Gabe stands before me, his black pants hanging low on his hips, drawing my attention to his well-defined waistline. The sight of his bare torso, with its taut muscles and defined lines, leaves me speechless. His left shoulder scars aside, his physique is just as enticing as I remember.

His eyes bore into me with an icy glare, revealing his annoyance. "Sara! This is highly inappropriate!" His words cut through the air like a knife. "Show some respect for my privacy!"

Taken aback by his tone, I feel a flicker of uncertainty within me. However, determined not to let it show, I straighten my posture and compose my thoughts. With a subtle shift of my weight and a firm yet measured tone, I find my voice again. "Gabe, we need to talk." I lift my chin to meet his gaze.

"We can discuss this at a more convenient time," he says, throwing a black shirt over his head and sliding his arms into its short sleeves.

Undeterred, I persist in expressing my concern. "I have noticed your absence from our sessions and would like an explanation."

His intense, green eyes continue to bore into me, almost penetrating my resolve. I stand firm, grounding myself with each step forward, feeling the floor beneath my soles. I have a responsibility in his journey to recovery. There is too much at stake to allow his momentary rudeness to sway me.

"Surely, you would like to keep your job," he says. His voice drops an octave with a menacing undertone as he delivers his veiled threat. The nerve of him!

His absence is already jeopardizing my work. If his lack of progress continues, not only will it raise questions about my competence, but it will also negatively impact the proposal's progress. If this situation persists, I stand to lose a lot more than just my job as Sara Jensen.

"No-show client? Well then, there is no job, is there?" Irritation colors my voice as I watch him adjust his shirt.

"I don't like your pushy techniques! That's my explanation! Now, please leave!"

Pushy techniques? He's being such a punk! Ten years and no memory, but he still has the ability to be completely unreasonable in serious situations. How infuriating! The exercises are for his well-being. He should push through them regardless of his mood.

"I don't accept that explanation." I shake my head slowly.

"That has nothing to do with me," he says as he turns away to grab his cane leaning by the side of his oversized bed.

On impulse, I dash to the bed and snatch his cane before he can get to it. With triumph, I fix a firm gaze on him. "When you're ready to take your healing seriously, come get this. I can help you so you don't need this anymore, but you have to do your part. Do not give up on yourself before we've even begun."

I hurry to the door, aiming to stop any chance for protest or for me to doubt my actions. However, as I reach the doorway, a sudden thud followed by a soft curse halts my steps.

I turn around, my eyes widening as I take in the sight of Gabe sprawled on the floor, his right leg tucked up under his weight. Without a moment's hesitation, my legs move faster than my thoughts, propelling me toward him.

I crouch down by his side and reach for him without thinking. I'm able to stop myself before touching him. "Are you all right, Gabe?" I ask, extending my hand toward him to offer my support and help him up.

He grumbles, brushing off my help at first, but accepts it grudgingly as he grasps my hand. "I'm fine," he mutters as he sits up, his warm and firm hand still holding mine. I am acutely aware of his proximity and want to prolong the moment. I can see every detail of his face, from the faint shadows beneath his lids to the squareness of his cheekbones. His lips slightly part. My heart skips a beat, and I yearn to meet them.

Wrong! I know thinking about someone else's husband like that is inappropriate, even if he is my ex-fiancé. Not that he remembers any of that. This mysterious wife remains a stranger to me. Uncertain, my chest tightens. I force myself to swallow, suppressing the lump forming in my throat.

I take a deep breath, remove my hand from his grip, stand up quickly, and step back, putting some space between us. I try to refocus us on the reason I'm here, the therapy. We have to address this situation now. We need a win-win solution.

"Gabe, I understand you may have reservations about the techniques I've been employing," I say, holding my voice steady. "I designed them for you."

He glances up at me, tilting his head back, causing his hair to cascade across his face. He looks undeniably sexy.

Shaking my head to ground myself, I continue more gently. "Your recovery requires effort and commitment from both of us. Let me help you."

His tense expression softens, and I take it as a sign that my words are reaching him. "I don't want to give up on you, Gabe. Let's make rehab more comfortable for you. We can make a plan together."

Silence hangs in the air for a moment as he contemplates my words. With a sigh, he nods. "All right." With the hostility in the air evaporating, relief washes over me. We've taken the first step toward bridging the gap and rebuilding trust. Although there is a long road ahead, his willingness to cooperate gives me hope for progress.

Gently, I retrieve his cane from where I dropped it when he fell, handing it back to him with a smile. "Consider this a symbol of our mutual commitment," I say.

He raises his hand to take the cane, exposing a patch on his right arm, red with a trickle of blood.

"You're bleeding!" I immediately crouch back down by his side and gingerly grab his arm.

"I didn't want to interrupt your heartfelt speech, so I refrained from informing you earlier. This is the reason I skipped the pool session." Gabe's calm demeanor doesn't waver as he acknowledges the inadequate plastic patch.

I swallow my retort that we're working on his leg, not his arm, and attempt to stay professional. "I have dry land alternatives." I turn my attention back to his injury. "You should have told me immediately. This needs proper attention."

He shrugs nonchalantly, downplaying the injury. "It's just a scratch. From that shelf, trying to fish out a book that slipped down the back. Nothing to fuss over."

"Gabe, it's not just a scratch. Neglecting even minor wounds can lead to complications. Trust me, I know."

A playful smile, a rarity of its kind, tugs at the corners of his lips, a glint in his eyes as he speaks. "I've been told to never trust a beautiful woman, Miss Jensen."

My breath hitches, and I can feel a subtle warmth spreading across my cheeks. I'm certain if Gabe looks at me, he will notice. Although there is no way to misunderstand his words–he clearly just told me I'm beautiful.

Thoughts quickly fill my mind. Is he flirting with me? It seems unlikely, considering that he has a daughter and likely a wife. My eyes instinctively shift to his hand, searching for a wedding ring. To my surprise, there is no band occupying any of his fingers.

Perhaps he removed the ring before his shower and hadn't put it back on since I interrupted him while he was getting dressed. That seems plausible, given the circumstances. Yet, despite my many interactions with Hugh and Katie, who always has her nose buried in a book, I can't recall ever hearing about a wife.

"Where's your wife?" The words slip out of my mouth before I can filter them through logic.

"My wife?"

The question lingers in the air, waiting for his response.

CHAPTER 5

Gabriel

"My wife?" I echo.

Sara's response catches me off guard. It seemingly came out of nowhere. Is this her way of trying to deflect my compliment? Or perhaps I left room for misinterpretation with my statement? I was aiming to ease the tension.

But out of all the topics she could have chosen for escape, why did she ask about my... wife? "Where's your wife?" Her words linger in the air, revealing her belief about my marital status.

A chuckle escapes from deep within me, gaining momentum until laughter rolls out of me, filling the space. It finally dawned on me that Sara's discomfort stems from the idea of me flirting while being married.

Sara clearly assumes I've lost my mind. She frowns at me, exasperated. "What's so funny?"

I'm amused by the situation, but I know I need to address her question seriously. It is ridiculously silly, though. My laughter slowly subsides, fading into an upward tug of my lips, and I meet Sara's eyes, attempting to compose myself and use a more appropriate tone.

"Sara, I assure you, I am not married," I begin. "There is no wife in the picture. I understand your concern, but I want to clarify that any friendly exchanges we've had are simply that–friendly."

Sara's features soften, settling into a more neutral expression as she processes my words. I wonder what is running through her head.

"I apologize if I misunderstood." Her voice lacks the intensity she had displayed when she had entered the room to confront me. "It's just that, well... it seemed like you were flirting, and I don't want to intrude on your personal life," she mutters under her breath, shifting her eyes around the room, clearly uncomfortable with the direction our conversation has taken.

I nod, acknowledging her explanation. "I appreciate your concern. It's understandable, given the circumstances. But do believe me."

With a faint smile, Sara straightens, seemingly pulling herself back together. It is astonishing how quickly she expresses and switches emotions. "Thank you for clarifying, Gabe. Now, shall we keep you from bleeding all over your bedroom?"

I won't admit it out loud, but I had momentarily forgotten about the bleeding cut. Her presence brings with it a new sort of inexplicable comfort.

"Of course. There is a medical kit in the bathroom," I inform her. The tension in the room dissipates with the sound of a cabinet opening as she finds the kit, quickly replaced by a renewed sense of focus on the task at hand.

Sara returns with the medical kit, placing it on my bed, her fingers gliding over the familiar contents with practiced ease. Every dip into the antiseptic solution and dab on my skin is executed with precision and deliberation.

As she works, I notice a subtle change in her demeanor. The lines of professionalism etched on her face become more pronounced. Her eyes linger on the area around my wound, studying it intently as if searching for any subtle nuances or signs of underlying damage. It has her full attention, her eyes never leaving the task at hand. She takes her role seriously, leaving no room for oversight. It's endearing.

Silence envelops us. The room seems to fade into the background, leaving only the sound of our breathing and the gentle swabs of the cleaning solution. With each careful motion, the ache in my injured skin gradually subsides, replaced by a subtle stinging.

As Sara finishes, she meets my gaze with a reassuring smile. "All done," she announces as she tapes the clear adhesive film over the wound. I didn't even know this high-tech dressing was in the kit.

"Thank you, Sara," I grasp her lingering hand as I find myself lost in her hazel eyes.

Her smile widens, a spark of warmth lighting her eyes. "You're welcome, Gabe," she replies.

"You have a beautiful smile. Have I mentioned..." my voice trails off, my attention now on the curve of her glossy lips. There is something magnetic about her. I feel it whenever I get close to her.

"Well, Gabe," she responds monotonously, her lingering grin giving her away. "I believe you've mentioned it once or twice, but it's always nice to hear it again," she admits playfully.

A grin plays on my lips as I lean in slightly, lowering my voice conspiratorially. "Ah, well, I can't help but appreciate the beauty that graces my presence."

Sara's cheeks flush faintly, a coy smile playing on her lips. "Is that still your way of being friendly, Gabe?" she quips, her voice laced with amusement.

I chuckle, appreciating her playful retort. "Touché," I admit, a mischievous glint in my eyes. "Perhaps I might have ventured into the realm of flirting." The overwhelming urge to kiss her has me leaning forward, brushing my thumb across her lower lip.

"Excuse me, Mr. Hartwell, sir," the voice of Katie's nanny, Mrs. Gregory, interrupts with urgency, and I drop my hand before it touches Sara's face. She enters the room, carrying Katie in her arms. The sight of Katie with tear-stained cheeks and tousled hair tells me she just woke up from another afternoon nap nightmare. My heart sinks at the sight, overwhelming me with guilt.

Quickly, I rise from the ground and reach out, pulling Katie into a tight embrace as she buries her face against my chest.

Stepping back, Sara gives us the space we need. As I look at the physical therapist, I realize I had forgotten not only basic courtesies but also the complexities of my life. Katie will always come first when she needs me.

As I cradle my daughter, whispering soothing words into her ear, a whirlwind of emotions churns inside me. My heart aches for Katie, and I yearn to ease her fears. "It's not real, princess," I murmur, hoping to provide some solace. However, despite my attempts, she continues to cry persistently.

If her mother, Ella, were here, she would likely have valuable insight on how to handle this situation. I am such a horrible person. I caused her to lose her family, and even now, I struggle to provide the comfort she needs during her episodes.

"May I?" Sara interjects abruptly, her voice interrupting my thoughts. "I have a son, and though it's not exactly the same, he also experienced nightmares after watching a horror film with no supervision." She pauses, realizing she is digressing. "Sorry, it's a long story, but..." She extends her hand toward Katie. To my surprise, Katie does not protest.

She has a son. I hadn't ever considered it. Perhaps she is the best person to help calm Katie.

"Hi there, my love," she coos. "Do you want to talk to Daddy's leg doctor about your bad dream? I'm here if you want to share."

A wave of anxiety courses through my body, making it thrum with unease. I can't understand why she would ask her to retell a nightmare. It would only serve to further upset her. Before I can even start voicing my concerns, Katie timidly begins to mumble, interrupting my train of thought.

"I was looking for my mommy, and there was this witch. She cut my hair and took Daddy's legs." As she continues recounting the incident, her sniffles gradually subside. "It was so scary," she adds, with a light cough.

Sara lightly pats Katie's back and snuggles her closer. "Oh my, you're so brave, Katie," she utters rather dramatically, prompting Katie to look up.

"I am?"

"You are. You faced a witch, and look," Sara's hand darts out, gingerly grabbing Katie's messy pigtail. "Your hair is still here." She shifts her gaze downward, pointing toward my legs. "And your daddy's short legs are right there." Her finger emphasized the length of my legs, catching me by surprise. Short legs?

Katie lets out a giggle, looking my way. "That is so brave of you," Sara continues. "Now, as a reward for your bravery, what snack would you like?"

"Cupcakes!" Katie enthusiastically exclaims. "And lots of icing?" she timidly adds as she glances at me. I swallow. I am concerned about her excessive sugar intake, but I can't find it in me to protest, not when she's looking at me with those sweet baby-blue eyes.

"You can have them all. Mrs. Gregory, please," I relent. "Thank you, Mrs. Gregory," I express my gratitude as she leaves the room to fetch Katie's requested snacks. With her departure, a sense of tranquility settles over the room, leaving only the hums of gentle breathing.

Sara shifts slightly, cradling Katie in her arms with the utmost care. The tenderness in her touch is evident as she pats down the messy strands of her hair.

"Gabe." Sara turns her attention back to me, her hazel eyes locking with mine. "I hope you know you're doing a great job as a father. Katie is lucky to have you."

Her words resonate deeply, stirring emotions I haven't fully acknowledged. "Thank you, Sara. I may falter in many aspects of my life, but Katie... Katie is my world," I confess, my voice betraying the raw emotion within.

Sara's eyes soften, mirroring the tenderness she displays toward Katie. "I can see that, and it's beautiful to witness."

Knowing that Sara recognizes the love I hold for my daughter, I feel relieved in a way. Maybe it was overly pessimistic of me to assume I was doing a terrible job as a father. I have a long way to go and grow for Katie, but I'm sure she would appreciate me doing my best rather than wallowing in past regrets.

We have a haunting and tragic past gripping not only my family but also countless other lives in its relentless hold. I lost the memories of my brother, Blake, and his wife, Ella. The accident itself is the only vivid recollection I have. Each day, I am burdened by the weight of their absence, with only the hollow echoes of their empty stares etched in my mind as a cruel and singular reminder of their existence.

I can vividly recall the scene before the accident: the illuminated cityscape casting a mesmerizing glow on the streets, my hands tightly gripping the leather-clad steering wheel, and a wave of nausea gently churning in the pit of my stomach. My older brother, Blake, had insisted that I stop driving after I started complaining of an upset stomach.

But I ignored his warning. The image of his concerned face flashed in my mind, asking me again to pull over so he could drive, but I brushed it aside. I don't remember what prompted it. However, I remember feeling it, the overwhelming cramp and pain and crashing against every fiber of my being. It left me gasping for breath, my body paralyzed in its grip right at the intersection with the bright green traffic. Apparently, I passed out from the pain with my foot on the accelerator. The car rode up the side of another car, was air borne and landed on the passenger side, where both Blake and Ella were sitting, took the full force of the impact.

Mrs. Gregory returns, carrying a tray adorned with the snacks we requested. Her presence snaps me out of the unsettling memory. Katie's eyes light up with delight as she catches sight of the treats, bringing a smile to my face. Sara gently releases Katie from her embrace and settles her on the edge of my bed.

"Here you go, my brave princess," Sara says affectionately as she hands Katie a cupcake. Katie eagerly begins munching on her treat, forgetting her earlier distress.

As Katie enjoys her treat, I am grateful for this momentary respite from her sadness. The room fills with the sweet scent of sugar, intertwining with the sound of her contented munching. Yet, in the back of my mind, I know that this fleeting happiness won't erase the challenges she faces. Treats alone can't whisk away the pain of missing her parents.

I glance at Sara and think maybe the presence of a motherly figure will help.

CHAPTER 6

Sydney

His intense gaze is making it quite challenging to focus on wiping the icing from Katie's face. Gabe's piercing stare has a knack for leaving me flustered, and I would much prefer his nonchalance. The sudden change in his demeanor triggers my memories of our shared past, which I have been trying to avoid.

Had I known he would impact me this deeply, I would have reconsidered visiting his bedroom to voice my concerns. But that would have deprived me of the joy of cheering up this little sweetheart.

As Katie eagerly devours the last bite of her cupcake, her cheeks puff out with each hurried bite. Concerned that she might choke, I watch her closely. I wonder when Gabe last allowed her to indulge in such sweets. Even during our college days, he was always against having them. It took a special occasion to entice him, the health freak that he was. And even then, he would limit his intake.

Katie extended her left palm, presenting a crumbly remnant of the cupcake. "Do you want some?"

A fleeting snicker escapes me as I gingerly pick it up. "Thank you, kind princess," I reply. Her sweet tooth must be a trait she inherited from her mother, whose identity Gabe has yet to reveal.

He insisted he wasn't married, but here stands his daughter, exhibiting the unmistakable Hartwell resemblance in her features. There must have been a wife at some point. He couldn't have brought her into the world alone.

I side-glance from feeding Katie and meet Gabe's eyes that are fixed on me once again. The secrecy surrounding his personal life sparks curiosity within me. Is he deliberately hiding his marriage from me? Or is there a deeper reason for his secrecy that I am missing?

Regardless, I consciously decide to set aside those thoughts for now. It isn't my place to pry, not as Sara Jensen nor as Sydney Pearce.

Just as Katie finishes the last bite, a subdued knock resonates through the open doorway. Hugh steps inside the room as immaculate as ever, his silver hair neatly combed to the side. "Excuse me, Mr. Hartwell," Hugh announces with smooth formality, "it's time for Miss Katie's afternoon lessons."

A modestly dressed, petite lady stands beside Hugh, seemingly ready to accompany Katie to her studies. She offers me a cordial smile before shifting her attention to the little girl. "Come along, Katie. We mustn't be late."

Katie leaves my side reluctantly, casting a longing glance at me as Mrs. Gregory steers her out of the room. She closes the door behind them, and a peaceful silence settles within the space.

In the stillness, I tidy up the remnants of Katie's sweet indulgence, the crumpled cupcake wrapper left on the bed. The muffled sound of my movements punctuated the room, the gentle rustle of cleaning up. The heaviness of the silence hangs in the air, filling the void between us. I side-glance at Gabe again. His expression is distant.

"Gabe," I finally speak, breaking the silence with a mellow tone, "Your daughter seems to have a strong liking for sweets. I'm sure she inherited your fondness for them."

My curiosity got the best of me. It isn't my place to pry, but playing dumb like this isn't really prying. I simply made a false observation, which I know Gabe will clarify because I know he is not fond of sweets.

"I'm not fond of sweets," he begins, pausing briefly before continuing. "It's more likely a trait inherited from her mother."

He took the bait. I was right. He did have a wife at some point. But why does he appear so pained? Had they experienced a bitter fallout?

"Or perhaps from my brother, her father," he reveals with a bitter sigh. "They're both dead, and I don't remember them well enough to know who Katie takes after."

At his words, my heart sinks. I had never known that Blake and Ella had a daughter. The revelation hits me like a cold tidal wave. Katie was his niece, yet he has taken on the responsibility of being her father. Even after essentially not knowing them or their daughter after the accident.

It would be inappropriate to press him further on the subject. He appears visibly uncomfortable, and it doesn't sit right with me that I had somewhat coerced him into opening up.

However, he continues, his voice heavy. "Do you want to know something funny?" He strides purposefully toward an intricately designed drawer stand and, with a swift motion, pulls open one of the drawers. As his hand disappears, a sense of anticipation fills the air.

"I don't remember them alive, but I do in death. Sometimes, I catch glimpses of that fateful night." His voice trembles slightly as he withdraws a photograph from the drawer. "Me behind the wheel, the crash, their lifeless eyes. It's as if their faces exist only within the confines of that tragedy. My only true memories of them."

His confession hangs solemnly in the air, suffocating the room. His eyes reflect the torment and burden he carries on his shoulders. It is a revelation that shatters the illusion of the tranquil life he had seemingly been living all these years. The formal facade he has maintained is now being stripped away, revealing a vulnerable man who remains haunted by his past.

What could have triggered this sudden pensiveness? He had been doing well until Katie's episode. Was Katie the trigger? Her nightmare?

I approach him slowly, taking measured steps toward him. "Gabe, you can't blame yourself for something you don't fully remember."

"I suppose," he mutters, shifting his body to face me. "But how can you tell I'm blaming myself?" He narrows his eyes, studying me intently.

Knowing Gabe as well as I do, it is evident that he is indeed blaming himself for the accident. The weight of guilt is etched across his features. However, explaining how I am able to discern his inner turmoil based on subtle facial cues—the crease in his dark brows, his downcast eyes—would undoubtedly be awkward. Not to mention, such an explanation risks jeopardizing my carefully guarded identity as Sara Jensen.

I offer a slight shrug, aware of the vagueness. "It's just a hunch," I admit, hoping to close the matter quickly. However, the furrow in his brow deepens, his annoyance becoming evident.

Gabe let out a soft hum before speaking. "I believe it is time for you to leave," he states calmly. With a straightened back, he strides toward the doorway, his posture regaining its composed demeanor. "Thank you for your assistance. Expect me for our next session," he adds, gesturing for me to leave.

"Very well," I respond, matching his detached tone. The professional air that had once enveloped us taking center stage once again. Without lingering, I swiftly depart, crossing the threshold of his bedroom and stepping into the elongated hallway that leads to my own bedroom. As I make my way through the corridor, I reflect on the change in dynamics between us.

Mere days ago, he appeared visibly irritated by my presence; now, he opened up to me about a deeply rooted trauma. This newfound vulnerability has revealed a side of Gabe that struck a chord within me, evoking memories of a sensitivity I had forgotten. Yet, as quickly as he allowed me in, he seemed to shut himself down again.

What is going on in his mind? And why am I so invested?

Seeking respite, I retreat to my bedroom, hoping our next interaction will at least yield fruitful results. The prospect compels me forward, eager to resume my work as soon as possible. I settle at the pristine white desk within the bedroom space, adorned with disheveled papers and an open laptop.

As my gaze fixes upon the blinking cursor on the laptop screen, a flurry of emotions washes over me: my role in Gabe's life as Sara Jensen is confined by the boundaries of our professional arrangement. Yet, deep within me, the essence of Sydney Pearce can't help but worry for him. How much is he shouldering by himself?

With a sigh, I redirect my attention to the task at hand, purposefully burying the perplexities that churn within me. My fingers gracefully dance across the keyboard, diligently crafting reports and analyzing the activities for his upcoming session.

And so, the day arrives, beckoning me to the poolside. Donned in swimwear and my hair neatly fastened in a bun, I approach the tranquil oasis. The placid water mirrors my unwavering determination to delve into the depths of Gabe's psyche.

As I stroll along, my hand instinctively reaches for my phone to check the time, only to feel it vibrate in my palm. Glancing at the screen, I notice it is a call from Brad, although it is unusual for him to call so early. However, as I answer, a wave of comfort washes over me upon hearing my son's voice.

"Hey, Mom," he greets, with faint rustling sounds in the background.

"Getting ready for your camping trip?" I inquire, already anticipating his response.

"Yup," he affirms, his words concise and to the point. "Just wanted to let you know I'm leaving now, and I love you."

A gentle smile claims my lips. "I love you too, sweetheart," I reciprocate. "Call me later when you arrive."

"Okay. Bye, Mom," he concludes, ending the call. Damon is never one for lengthy conversations, often reaching out simply to relay a quick message.

A pang of longing surges through me. I would have loved to personally prepare him for his camping trip, but perhaps it is necessary for him to spend more time with Brad. Ever since the divorce, although they still have lots of fun together, their relationship has become strained at times, and my concern for my dear son has grown. I don't want him to be without a father figure.

Regaining my composure, I shift my attention back toward the pool, where Gabe has already immersed himself. Despite the lingering lightness from the conversation with my son, duty beckons.

Approaching the cool edge of the blue-tiled pool, I offer a smile as I greet him. "You're early today," I say in an attempt to make small talk with him.

His deep emerald gaze briefly meets mine, but he remains mute, focused solely on the movements of his legs in the water. Is he purposefully ignoring me?

Shaking my head, I dismiss the thought. Surely, he wouldn't, he has no reason to. He is just being his usual grumpy self this early in the morning.

Sitting down on the edge of the pool, I carefully dip my feet into the water. A rush of cool moisture quickly envelopes my feet, spreading to the rest of my body as I lower myself in.

Minutes pass, and with the growing heavy silence, it becomes quite clear that my initial assessment wasn't mistaken. Gabe is deliberately ignoring me! And his avoidance of meaningful conversation is deeply frustrating. His curt nods and sharp hums, which he seems to think are appropriate responses, make it exceedingly difficult to gauge his progress with the exercises. What exactly is his problem?

Gabe's behavior has become increasingly erratic and unpredictable. The more I try to understand him, the farther he seems to drift from the Gabe I once knew.

Or maybe I'm the problem? Expecting him to remain the same as I remember him? It has been a decade since we last interacted, and people can change significantly in that span of time, even without memory loss.

But how far can one stray from their former self? It is truly unsettling, the thought of losing him altogether. I have never truly accepted his sudden disappearance from my life. Perhaps this is the wake-up call I need to confront my feelings.

A lump forms in my chest, and tears threaten to spill from my eyes. I blink them back, trying to maintain neutrality as I observe him floating in the water, legs flailing and splashing about.

He is fortunate in a way, not burdened by the memories of our past shared experiences, free to live without the knowledge of them weighing on him.

Perhaps it is time to release myself from the burden of our past. Moving forward, I decide I will fully dedicate myself to my role as Sara Jensen, focusing on my work and seizing the opportunity to expand PTX. My ultimate goal is to create a fulfilling life for myself and my son, Damon.

Gabe, my ex-fiancé with no memory of me, now holds a different position in my life—he is merely a client.

CHAPTER 7

Sydney

"You will never give Gabriel a moment's peace, will you? Two years, and you still suffocate him," Larissa Hartwell spat, her face holding a monotonous expression as she loomed over me, her words colored with malice.

Of all the hurtful opinions she had shared, those words had stung the most. On the day of the NHL draft, I had been involved in a running accident during a race at that left me in crutches. Closely packed competitive runners, it's not the first time. As soon as the draft was over, instead of celebrating being chosen in the second round, Gabe came looking for me.

It was a sweet gesture. However, his mother vehemently disapproved. Needless to say, I had given up on ever winning Larissa Hartwell over after her one brief visit to my hospital room.

Gabe is finally making noticeable progress. Earlier this week, Gabe informed me that his parents would be visiting soon to see for themselves, and I should meet them. I hid my dread and wished "soon" would mean weeks.

"Please prepare yourself to welcome Mr. and Mrs. Hartwell later this afternoon. They'll be here for a week, staying in the north wing," Hugh relays before discreetly exiting my bedroom.

While I had never met Arnold Hartwell, Gabe's father, Larissa certainly knew me well enough. One look at me, and she would instantly recognize that I was not Sara Jensen but Sydney Pearce, the poor scholarship riffraff who had supposedly seduced her youngest son.

In short, I am royally screwed. How had I never considered the possibility of encountering Gabe's mother? I have grown accustomed to seeing only Gabe and Katie as the prominent members of the Hartwell family, completely disregarding the existence of his pompous parents.

What am I going to do? Will she even recognize me? It has been well over ten years, and my appearance has changed since my twenties. But she might recognize me and remember me the way she had always seen me: the social climber lucky enough to capture her son's attention.

I sigh heavily, massaging the light tension between my brows. There is no use in getting more frustrated by worrying. The solution is quite simple.

I will let my long hair fall loosely over my face and wear my reading glasses. Jane had once told me how different I look with them on. Perhaps a slight alteration in my appearance will yield a favorable outcome. Adding a touch of makeup, albeit subtly, wouldn't hurt either. Larissa Hartwell may also be shallow enough that she has forgotten about me.

After determining my plan of action, I sift through my wardrobe, rummaging for something suitable to wear when welcoming a client's parents. After settling on a loosely fitted chiffon blouse and a pair of long black pants, I comb my hair to fall sideways across my face, subtly obscuring my features.

With a touch of makeup and my glasses perched on my nose, my appearance takes on a noticeably different aura than my usual self. After slipping into a pair of pumps that perfectly match my pants, I grab my phone and exit the bedroom, ensuring to lock the door behind me.

I am ready to face Larissa Hartwell.

The walk down the hallway to the living room is quiet, with only the clicking of my heels on the marble breaking the silence. Glancing at my phone for the time, I realize I might be ready a bit too early—it was just approaching noon.

Exhaling deeply, I slow my pace, allowing my footsteps to tarry. Truth be told, I have nothing to do at the moment. Gabe's session for the day had already taken place, and as it had for the past week, he remained adamant about maintaining his distance and keeping our conversations brief.

Not that I am bothered by it. What occasionally troubles me are the lingering glances I catch when he thinks I'm not looking and the distant look in his eyes when they do meet mine. It triggers an unsettling feeling in the pit of my stomach.

A mild tugging at the right side of my blouse catches my attention, and I instinctively look down to find the source. I blink in surprise at the sight before me. When had she arrived? "Katie!" I exclaim, noticing the small girl at my side, her petite fingers clutching the fabric of my blouse, her lips quivering.

Something was wrong. I tenderly hold her hand, cradling it in my free palm as I crouch down to meet her gaze. "What's wrong, princess?" I inquire as softly as possible.

She sniffs, pursing her lips into a deep frown. How cute! I suppress the urge to giggle at her adorable display of annoyance.

As I am comforting Katie, our moment is abruptly interrupted by a familiar voice calling behind me. "Katie, my darling! There you are!" The pitch of the voice immediately grabs my attention, and I turn in its direction.

Approaching us with the grace and poise befitting a woman of her status is Larissa Hartwell, Gabe's mother. Her usually fair hair is elegantly styled into a bun, and its darker shade beautifully contrasts with her flawless complexion. She is wearing a stunningly tailored white dress that accentuates her regal presence.

Walking by her side is her husband, Arnold Hartwell, a tall and distinguished older man with a salt-and-pepper beard that adds to his elegant aura of wealth.

"Granny!" Katie exclaims, her blue eyes shimmering at the sight of her grandmother. Larissa beams affectionately, her wrinkles crinkling to highlight a wide smile as she reaches out to embrace Katie, momentarily diverting her attention from whatever had been troubling her before her grandmother's arrival.

My heart races within my chest, anxiety simmering beneath the surface as Larissa abruptly shifts her attention toward me. I plaster a warm smile on my face, striving to maintain composure despite the nerves bubbling within. "Mrs. Hartwell, Mr. Hartwell, it is a pleasure to meet you both," I greet them, extending my hand.

Larissa's gaze visibly scrutinizes me for a moment, her piercing eyes seeming to search for something as they move up and down my figure. Yet, I maintain my composure and resolve to conceal my true identity. "Sara Jensen, is it?" she inquires as she shakes my hand.

I nod, my voice steady. "Yes, ma'am."

Larissa's expression curves into a puzzled look. "Have we met before?" She leans closer, lowering her voice.

A shiver of unease runs through my skin, leaving goosebumps in its wake. How can she be sensing familiarity? My disguise should be enough to convince her otherwise.

"I don't believe so," I quickly respond, playing the flattery card. "I would not forget meeting someone as esteemed as you." Surprisingly, she takes my comment in good humor, responding with a chuckle.

"Indeed," she remarks.

"Has Mr. Hartwell mentioned his remarkable progress in his physical therapy sessions?" I smoothly redirect the conversation, knowing well enough that she will take the bait. She is likely interested in her son's well-being.

However, Arnold Hartwell is the one who responds, nodding with approval, his deep voice carrying an air of authority. "Yes, it is truly impressive, considering his recovery had stalled for so long. We owe his progress to your exceptional skills, Miss Jensen."

I humbly accept his praise, carefully concealing my inner anxiety. "Thank you, Mr. Hartwell. It's been an honor to support your son in his rehabilitation. He has displayed incredible resilience."

I may be slightly exaggerating. Gabe's progress in the past week is primarily evident in his increased tolerance for the lingering discomfort in his left knee, particularly during more strenuous movements in the pool. But progress is progress.

Larissa's eyes shimmer slightly, her lashes delicately fluttering. "Well, we should celebrate. How about joining us for dinner tonight, Miss Jensen? We would be delighted to have the opportunity to get to know you better, especially considering the support you have provided to Gabriel during this challenging period."

Her invitation catches me off guard, and I can perceive she is subtly hinting at something, though I'm not quite sure what. Masking my surprise, I respond, "I would be honored, Mrs. Hartwell. It would be a pleasure to join you for a meal and further discuss Gabriel's progress," I say, emphasizing my intentions for accepting the dinner invitation.

Larissa's smile widens, indicating her satisfaction with my reply. "Wonderful! We will expect you at the dining table at eight o'clock," she concludes our conversation gracefully.

"Come on, Katie, darling," Larissa gently beckons to Katie, who had been quietly observing our exchange. As they turn to leave, Larissa's hand rests tenderly on Katie's shoulder. I release a long exhale, my palm finding its place on my chest, calming my frayed nerves.

The evening ahead holds a pivotal encounter, testing my ability to maintain my facade. I will have to navigate the intricate dance of conversation, concealing my true identity, all while ensuring that Gabe's progress remains the focal point of our conversation. I'm sure it will be an absolute headache.

After another deep breath, I nod to myself, ready to confront the challenge head-on. A thought pricks at my conscience, a hint of disappointment over not uncovering the cause of Katie's earlier distress. I reassure myself that there will be an opportunity to address it later, seeking solace in the privacy of my room as I retreat.

Taking a seat in the comfortable armchair at my cluttered desk, where my laptop and disheveled paperwork lay, I allow my mind to wander. The mere presence of Larissa Hartwell has me on edge, causing me to question my ability to maintain my carefully crafted facade as Sara. Concealing my true identity is paramount, no matter what it takes. The stakes are too high, and I can't afford to make a single mistake.

In an attempt to distract myself from the impending dinner, I reach for my phone and dial my ex-husband's number, hoping to speak with my son.

"Sydney," Brad begins, his voice filled with concern.

I smile, knowing exactly what he wants to ask. "I'm doing well. Please don't worry."

"It's hard not to worry when it comes to you," he retorts. The word "liar" tarries on my tongue, but I hold it back. Arguing will only drain my energy, and I don't want Damon to witness any tension. The divorce has offered quite enough of that already.

"Damon, it's your mom calling," Brad's voice booms through the speaker, unaware of how loud he yelled for Damon in the other room, making me flinch.

"Mom?" Damon's voice gently interrupts my thoughts, providing a welcome respite from the weight of my worries.

"Hello, sweetie," I greet him warmly. After exchanging affectionate pleasantries, Damon eagerly regales me with tales of his camping trip, recounting his adventures and challenges during the past week.

Listening to Damon go on about his life was a comforting interlude. Being away from him, away from our routine, has been difficult. We engage in a lively conversation, indulging in the joy of discussing even the silliest of things.

Just as we get immersed in our exchange, an audible double knock disrupts the moment. I glance at the door, taken aback by the unexpected intrusion. Hugh enters, holding a large black shopping bag adorned with what I recognize to be a luxury label.

"Hey, sweetie, I have to go now. I'll call you soon, okay?" I say. After Damon's affirmative response, I end the call.

"Mr. Gabriel requested that I deliver this to you," Hugh explains, gesturing for me to collect the bag.

I accept the package, offering a quick "Thank you, Hugh" before he steps out the door.

With caution and a dash of curiosity, I dip my hand into the bag, grasping the soft fabric and pulling it out to reveal an exquisite navy dress. The clothing is elegant, tailored to perfection, and exudes sophistication.

Confusion washes over me as I ponder why Gabe had taken the initiative to provide me with appropriate attire for the evening.

He ignores me all week, and suddenly, he's sending me a dress to wear to dinner with his parents. My mind swirls with questions as I stare at the dress in my hands. Why has Gabe sent it? Is it a gesture of reconciliation or an attempt to appease his parents by ensuring I am appropriately dressed for dinner?

I suppose there is only one way to find out.

CHAPTER 8

Gabriel

The mouth-watering aroma of dinner fills the air, making my stomach growl with hunger. My mother has organized another one of her elaborate dinners. These gatherings always bring her immense joy, and this time, she's using Sara Jensen as the reason to host such an event.

Despite my ongoing pretense of relishing our lack of communication, I don't wish to place Sara in an uncomfortable position during tonight's affair. When Hugh informed me about the dinner, it felt appropriate to arrange attire for Sara. I was sure she hadn't anticipated such an event, and I want her to feel at ease and adequately prepared. As for why I want this, I can't quite articulate it. I simply add it to the list of perplexing sentiments I harbor for Sara Jensen.

With measured steps, I draw nearer to the dining table, where my parents sit, accompanied by several bottles of wine. I had instructed Mrs. Gregory to exclude Katie from tonight's dinner, as it appeared likely to extend past her bedtime, and the nature of the discussions would likely fail to entertain her.

I settle into my seat, taking in the display before me. The mahogany table, polished to a lustrous sheen, stands at the center of the dining room, adorned with a white lace tablecloth delicately embroidered with rose floral patterns. On the table are fine china plates, gleaming silverware, and crystal wine glasses that catch the soft golden glow of the chandelier above. Intricately arranged floral centerpieces, bursting with vibrant hues, add a touch of natural beauty to the scene.

As I adjust my position, my parents glance at me, concern etched in their eyes. It is their custom to inquire about my well-being during such occasions, but tonight, I anticipate their questions will be met with a well-crafted lie. I have grown skilled in masking the truth, for the complexities of my internal struggles are not ones I wish to share openly with them.

Father is the first to ask this time, his voice full of paternal worry. "How have you been, Gabriel? You look tired."

A wistful smile plays on my lips as I reply, "It is merely the weight of growing responsibilities at Hartwell Enterprises."

"You're doing well, son. Blake was groomed to run Hartwell, not you. You'll be able to take over before the year is out. You've done very well, and I'll be able to step back."

Blake. My guilt returns. Blake was to have been CEO three years ago. He and my dad had been working towards that timeline. A rare acknowledgement of Blake from my dad. Our stoic family. Thank goodness we have Katie or it'd be as if Blake and Ella never existed.

Mother reaches for a wine bottle, gracefully pouring a generous amount into my glass. "How has your week been here? Are your sessions going well?"

She's changing the subject, like always.

I take a sip of wine, suppressing a wince as the bitter liquid touches my tongue. "Yes, Mother, the sessions are going well," I reply, keeping my tone steady, wrestling with both my guilt as well as my PT progress.

This isn't entirely true, but I can't bring myself to burden them with the reality of my situation. The pain is still a constant companion, no matter how much progress I try to show.

Father interjects, "And what about your dizzy spells?"

I nod, aiming to alleviate their worries. "They have become less frequent," I reply, hoping that is enough.

As the interrogations unfold, my thoughts gravitate toward Sara Jensen. There is still so much I long to discover about her, particularly the familiarity that resonates within me. It occurs to me that my parents might hold some insight, and they can't possibly lie straight to my face, so I decide to take this opportunity to inquire discreetly about her.

"There's something I've been meaning to ask you," I begin, feigning casual curiosity, cutting their inquires short. "Sara Jensen. Have either of you come across her before you hired PTX?"

As she responds, my mother's eyes shimmer with intrigue, her tone carefully measured. "Not that I recall. Why do you ask?"

Very odd. From her careful tone, I realize they may have, and likely have, withheld that information even if they were acquainted with her. It wouldn't be the first time they kept a secret from me. But I had anticipated a different response. However, their knowledge of Sara Jensen, if any, is likely intertwined with the hidden truths they hold close.

"No reason," I reply, masking my curiosity behind a neutral expression. "She seems vaguely familiar to me, as if I had met her in passing. But perhaps it is just my imagination."

My mother's lips curve into a thoughtful smile. "It is possible, dear. Sometimes, faces can trigger false memories or associations. Sara Jensen must have subconsciously reminded you of someone else."

I nod, accepting her explanation, although my intuition hints at a deeper truth. For now, I decide to let the matter rest. Sara Jensen will remain a mystery to me, at least for now.

I wonder when she will join us. My gaze drifts toward the hallway, and as if summoned, a figure appears at the threshold, clad in the very dress I had purchased for her.

My heart quickens, seemingly eager to catch up to the sudden surge of emotions within me. Her dark hair cascades in loose waves, partially obscuring her face, adding an air of allure. Every movement she makes, every step she takes, every sway of her hips seems to be imbued with a grace and poise that has me in a chokehold.

Her arrival seems to lift the weight of the room and infuse it with an unexpected cheeriness. A smile creeps onto my lips, betraying the swirl of emotions coursing through me. It is as if a ray of sunlight has penetrated the dark corners of my existence.

The feeling is truly perplexing.

"I do hope I'm not late." Sara's voice carries a hint of anxiousness, striking a chord deep within me. Is she uncomfortable in the dress?

I quickly gather my composure and respond, "Not at all, Sara. You're right on time. Please, have a seat."

With effortless grace, Sara moves toward the vacant chair beside me. Her steps are light, her smile radiant. As she settles into her seat, my parents' eyes light up with genuine warmth and curiosity.

My mother leans forward, her eyes sparkling with delight. "Sara, it's a pleasure to speak with you further. Gabriel has told us so much about your skills as a physical therapist. We've been quite intrigued."

Sara's laughter dances through the air like a delicate melody. "Oh, you're serious." She coughs lightly, shooting me a quick, perplexed look. "With the way Gabriel glares at me during our sessions, it would make you think I was rather torturing him. It's nice to know he has good things to say about me."

My father chuckles, a twinkle in his eyes. "Ah, yes, our Gabriel has always had a knack for making things look way more dramatic than they are."

A blush tinges my cheeks as I cough lightly. I certainly do not. I glance at Sara, my heart skipping a beat at the sight of her laughter. Her eyes meet mine for a fleeting moment before abruptly shifting away.

As Hugh quietly enters the dining area, accompanied by two maids pushing trolleys of food, the enticing aroma fills the air. The dishes are an exquisite array of flavors and colors, a feast far beyond appropriate for this uneventful occasion. I resist the urge to sigh.

My parents, ever the gracious hosts, eagerly converse with Sara, their genuine interest evident in their smiles and attentive gazes. Sara effortlessly charms them, her apparent charisma shining through as she shares stories of her physical therapist experiences and interactions with various patients.

As we enjoy the delectable dishes, my attention occasionally drifts to Sara. I observe the grace with which she holds her cutlery, her delicate gestures as she expresses herself, and the way her eyes sparkle with delight. Her presence adds a touch of mystery to the evening, a mystery I plan on unraveling.

As the evening progresses, our plates empty, and the conversations gradually transition to lighter topics, mostly between my parents.

"Thank you for the beautiful dinner, Mr. Hartwell, Mrs. Hartwell," Sara suddenly speaks up, drawing my attention from my nearly finished plate of decadent chocolate pâté.

"But I'm afraid I have to retire to bed now to be ready for tomorrow's early session," she explains, pushing her seat back as she stands up.

"Oh my. Thank you for making this dinner splendid, Sara. We appreciate you joining us," my mother said, offering her a warm smile.

I watch Sara walk away, gradually fading out of sight down the hallway. I rarely have the opportunity to engage in real conversation with her, and I realize it is a consequence of my earlier dismissals of her attempts to engage with me.

Why have I been avoiding talking to her? After she assisted me with Katie and provided consolation when I opened up about the accident, I can't fathom why I had nonchalantly pushed her away amid her support. Apologizing to her seems like the right course of action, a necessary step to rectify my behavior and show her the respect she deserves.

"Well, I have to attend that early session too. I should also head for bed. Father, good night. Mother, thank you. A splendid meal as always."

A sense of urgency surges through me. I hurry toward Sara's room. The corridor stretches endlessly ahead of me, each step burdened by the weight of my intentions. Finally reaching her door, doubt begins to gnaw at my mind.

It is late; perhaps it would be better to apologize in the morning. I hesitate, ready to turn away, but an inexplicable longing compels me to knock. Inhaling deeply, I lightly tap my knuckles against the door, my heart thudding in my chest. It has been far too long, and Sara Jensen always seems to be the catalyst.

Moments slip by, followed by the sound of shuffling, until the door gradually opens, revealing Sara's silhouette before me. Her hair now elegantly gathered in a loose bun, accentuating the graceful curve of her neck. She's still wearing the dress, its fabric contouring her figure in alluring ways.

I shake my head, dismissing the explicit thoughts probing the corners of my mind, suggesting sinful ideas in their wake.

"Gabe!" Her eyes widen, surprise coloring her soft voice. "Is there something I can help you with?"

I clear my throat, momentarily captivated by her appearance. "May I come in? I'd like to talk to you."

A momentary pause, then a small smile graces her lips as she steps aside, gesturing for me to enter. "Certainly, please come in."

Stepping into her room, the atmosphere shifts instantly. Soft lighting and cozy furnishings create an intimate ambiance that mirrors the growing tension between us. Taking a moment to gather my thoughts, I turn toward Sara, who is now facing me.

"I wanted to apologize," I begin. "I realized I've been rather unreasonable since..." I pause and swallow, the bitter taste of my words trying to discourage me from going further. "Since our conversation about the accident."

Sara's expression softens, her eyes reflecting understanding. "It's all right, Gabe. I understand you've been going through a lot. We all have our moments of uncertainty."

I nod, appreciating her empathy. "But that doesn't excuse my distant behavior toward you."

Her gaze locks with mine as if searching for something. "I'm not sure why you feel the need to apologize, Gabe," she murmurs, moving to sit at the edge of her bed and crossing her legs.

I can't help but question myself silently. Why do I feel the need to apologize? Do I really want to? Or is the apology merely an excuse to see Sara Jensen?

I pause, grappling with my thoughts. Yes, I want to see her, but it's more than that. Something is pulling me toward her, an unspoken bond–the enchanting gaze of her hazel eyes, the allure of her wavy hair, and the enticing aura she exudes. In that moment, the room seems to fill with an undeniable energy, an anticipation as I gaze at her. It is as if the room itself is holding its breath, awaiting the delicate transformation unfolding before its very walls.

CHAPTER 9

Sydney

"You're staring, Gabe," I blurt out. The words slip past my lips before I can filter them. It is true, though. Gabe is staring. Quite intently, too, and I frankly had too much wine to pretend not to notice. While not entirely intoxicated, I am undoubtedly tipsy. I had consumed enough wine to fuel my recklessness. Which is why I let him enter my room tonight, eager to hear whatever he had to say.

He had apologized, but what for? I'm not quite sure. He has every right to keep his distance or not. The choice is always his, and I can't fathom why he believes I might be offended. On the contrary, his actions have helped me realize what truly matters beyond the relationship we once shared.

"I can't help myself, Sara," he mutters under his breath, shifting to look at my desk, still so messy. How embarrassing!

But what does he mean by that? Is he flirting with me again? How cheeky. A burst of soft laughter escapes my lips.

"I suppose it is cheeky," he replies, his hands grazing the papers scattered across the desk as he speaks.

Did I say that out loud? I really am tipsy.

He chuckles softly, and a surge of emotional memories rushes through my chest, causing my breath to hitch. Had he just laughed? Had he done so at any point during the past two weeks I've spent here?

"I didn't know you could laugh again." I march to his side. I retrieve the papers from his grasp and swiftly gather the rest on the desk, aligning them with care.

"Again? You speak as if you've witnessed me laughing before." He fixes his gaze upon me, his silence urging me to respond. I choose to ignore him.

Of course, I had seen him laugh before. I had witnessed his tears, his anger, and his vulnerability, each revealing a different facet of his character that I had embraced wholeheartedly despite any particularities.

I had been his girlfriend for three years and fiancée for a year. I had watched parts of his life in its entirety—his routines, his meals, his sleep, his passions, his phases–the start of some and the end of others. I loved him deeply. However, he had lost all memory of our shared experiences, and revealing our truth would only inflict pain on us both with no actual resolution.

"You must have misheard me," I assert, preparing to walk away from the desk. But just as I make my move, Gabe's firm grip on my hand stops me in my tracks.

My heart goes into a frenzy as I struggle to breathe, the tension in the air growing dense, and my mind only registering the tingling sensation of his palm on my skin. Why is he doing this? I had recently begun to come to terms with our reality, but now his presence is stirring up the emotions I had resolved to leave untouched.

I can't handle this, not right now.

"I don't believe so." He inches closer behind me, his tall, robust frame pressing against my back. His fingers delicately trace the skin of my hand to the edge of my shoulder, leaving goosebumps in their wake.

"Gabe," I breathe out, my voice colored with desperation, shocking even myself. Please, I want to say, please leave. But the words don't feel genuine. Do I truly want him to go?

"What are you hiding from me, Sara?" he whispers by my left ear, his breath grazing my skin, causing my breath to catch and my heart to thrum in my chest.

I spin my body to face him, meeting his intense green gaze. The space between us crackles with heat, his rich scent invading my nose as I breathe him in. He smells of chocolate and wine.

His other hand leaves mine and cups my face, his palm rough, yet his touch remains tender as his fingers delicately rest on my skin.

"I'm not hiding anything, Gabe," I whisper back to him, hoping he doesn't catch the shakiness of my voice.

His lips part slightly, and I can't help but shift at the sight of them. They tempt me, calling me to meet them with mine so desperately. It has been far too long.

His thick thumb traces a path along my cheekbone, his eyes scrutinizing me. "Then, why do you feel so familiar?" he whispers, his voice deep, sending vibrations through my body.

At that moment, as his warm breath fans the skin of my face, my emotions churn within the confines of my beating heart. The walls I built trying to protect myself from the pain of our lost connection, along with my resolve and sanity, begin to crumble.

Without thinking it through, I lean closer, closing the gap between us. Our lips meet in a tentative kiss, a spark igniting a fire that had been smoldering for far too long. As I surrender to the magnetic pull drawing us together, the world around us fades into insignificance.

I place my hands on his chest, grasping his shirt tightly between my fingers. It feels surreal to have his lips on mine, and a part of me wonders if I'm simply having a very realistic dream.

The tip of his tongue brushes my lower lip, and I part them for him. The thrill of the familiar warmth and taste of him rushes through me. I run my hands around his neck, and my fingers gently entwine in his dark tresses, lightly tugging at their roots. His groan is lost in my mouth, and I shiver in response to the low noise, pulling him closer as he breaks the kiss, his teeth dragging my lower lip slowly.

"Why do I know you?" His question is breathless, his eyes searching mine, and I shake my head, pulling his lips back to my own. I can't answer that question. I shouldn't be doing this, but everything in me is desperate for more.

I feel his heart pounding against his chest, against mine, taking over the beat of my own, igniting a surge of electricity that courses through my veins. Slowly, we shift, moving backward until the back of my legs hit the edge of my bed. My arms tighten around his neck, and he bends lower for me, just as unwilling to break the kiss as I am.

His hot hands explore the contours of my body, the feel of his touch sending warmth between my legs, awakening an ache I hadn't experienced since before I lost him.

The kiss grows more urgent, our tongues intertwine, and my fingers find the buttons of his shirt, undoing them one by one. He presses forward, and my knees buckle, sending me falling onto the bed. He follows, the kiss breaking with his heady laugh.

My fingers are trembling as I undo the last button, peeling the shirt off his shoulders and revealing the expanse of his bare chest. He pulls away to take off the shirt entirely, letting it hit the floor.

I look up at him as he towers over me, but he pauses, hesitating as his eyes search mine. I don't know if he's looking for permission or answers, but he can't stop; I won't survive if he does. I press myself up, meeting his lips again with an eager urgency, hoping he can taste how much I want him.

He groans again, that low, vibrating tone reciprocating the same eagerness, taking my breath away as his arms curl around me and hold me tightly to his body. His hand slowly traces a path up my spine before settling on the nape of my neck. Gently, he loosens my dress, the fabric cascading off my shoulders, slowly baring my body to him as he drags the zipper down my back.

He pulls back again, only to lean to the side, and his lips find my shoulder. His teeth drag lightly along my collarbone, chasing my retreating dress as his mouth descends on my breast.

The warmth of his tongue swells across my nipple, the thumb of his other hand teasing the other, and I moan, arching into him.

My heart swells with feelings I can't discern, memories of our past flooding my mind. His breath tickles my skin as his mouth switches to my other breast.

Color dances behind my closed lids, goosebumps shivering to life on my skin as his lips graze back up between my breasts. I run my fingers through his tousled hair, pulling his head closer to me, relishing the feel of his beautiful mouth against my bare skin. Our bodies intertwine, fitting together like interlocking puzzle pieces, their warmth and contours blending seamlessly, just like they had done long ago.

His lips, growing possessive, graze my neck, leaving a trail of fiery kisses that stir every fiber of my being. My hands find the button of his slacks, his zipper, as his fingers hook the edge of my underwear and give a small tug. The clumsiness in both of us makes us laugh, our foreheads resting together, our breaths mingling as he pushes his pants and boxers free. I lift my hips, letting the lace drop to the floor.

He's between my legs, and his fingers brush my slit, pressing between my lower lips. His palm meets the tight bundle, and I grab his wrist.

"Please," my voice is breathless as I arch up against his hand, "I need you."

A breath shudders out of him like he's been struck by my words, and as his lips claim mine. I can feel the heat of his cock as it replaces his fingers, a long, slow stroke as he positions his hips.

My heart is thundering in my ears, knocking against my ribs like it's trying to break free. He holds my hips, pushing his length into me, and my heart skips a hard beat, stealing my breath. I cry out, arching up to meet him, wrapping my legs around his waist, and he eases one down, holding it in place as his hips move torturously slow.

He wants to savor, and I want him to consume. I'm greedy for the flood of memories, to feel them in real time again.

I squeeze my thighs, arching my lower back, and he thrusts once, hard, hilting inside of me, and it knocks the air from my lungs in a sound that risks being half a sob, so I cover my mouth. The emotions threaten to bubble out of me, and I know I can't let him see. I wrap my arm around his neck, pulling him closer, and he plants his hands on either side of my shoulders, bowing his head as his warm breath fans my neck. I squeeze my inner muscles, and his answering groan is like a starter pistol ringing in the air.

With each thrust, the connection between our bodies grows stronger, fueling the building tension within me. When he pulls my hand from my mouth, pinning it down to the bed above my head, I gasp, and his tongue delivers his taste to mine once again.

He thrusts harder, jerking my body under his, each stroke short, deep, and hitting every delicious nerve inside of me.

The kiss breaks, his fingers lacing with mine, his gaze meeting my own, demanding wordlessly with his panting breaths. I can hear his voice in my head from the past, telling me to come with him under that same gaze.

I squeeze his hand, and he shortens his thrusts more, deep, hot, stunting my breaths, and when he drives the final thrust home, my orgasm explodes like starlight behind my closed eyes. My body goes rigid, and his teeth find my shoulder again, biting, his lips moving up to whisper praise I can't decipher against my ear. I shiver in delight as his heat fills me and spills over in the last, weaker thrusts as he empties himself inside of me.

The sound of our ragged breathing gradually subsides as I hold him lazily, limbs heavy with pleasure and exertion. I feel myself drifting off as he lays beside me, curling his arms around my body. The softness of the bed envelopes us, and the sheets against our skin add to the haze of serenity of the moment.

Before giving in to sleep, I gaze up at Gabe, his long lashes fluttering as he drifts off, his chest rising and falling with each breath. With a content smile, I let myself fall asleep, too, knowing regardless of whether our encounter was a dream or not, I am very much okay with it.

Or so I thought.

I awaken, finding myself lying in a small bed, dressed in a hospital gown, surrounded by dim lighting. Tears streaming down my face as the weight of loneliness and heartache bears heavily on my shoulders. Clutching my stomach, I long for Gabe's presence, yearning for his comforting words, anything to ease my pain.

"Why isn't he here?" I whisper, my voice trembling with anguish, addressing the faceless nurse standing beside my bed. "When I need him the most?"

Anger courses through my veins, intensifying with each passing second. The realization striking me like a blow—he isn't coming. Gabe has forgotten me, forgotten everything about who I am. The injustice of it all ignites a fire within me, fueling my anger, resentment, and frustration. I can't understand why I have to go through this alone. Gabe is supposed to be here with me. This is supposed to be one of the most important moments of our lives together.

Suddenly, a scream tears through my lungs. The scene shifts, and I find myself back in the present, my eyes snapping open to meet Gabe's gaze of concern.

"What's wrong?" he asks, his voice full of anguish, his brow creasing on his forehead.

I hesitate, torn between past and present, between pushing him away to appease my anger and pulling him close, longing for his presence. But the overpowering ache of the memory fueling my anger decides for me.

"I need you to leave," I order him, trying to keep my voice free of the violent emotions brewing inside me.

It was a plea disguised as an order, a desperate attempt to shield myself from the suffocating pain. His concerned expression only adds to my frustration.

Gabe's face falls, and he begins to speak, "Sara, I..."

My ears shut down as my mind screams at me from inside. I am not Sara. I am Sydney! Sydney, the woman you loved and who loved you wholeheartedly. The woman you moved on from without even realizing it. The woman you left behind with all our memories together and our hopes for the future. Sydney, your fiancée! We were supposed to be married, to face the challenges of life together. I was ready to meet all of your family, the ones you cherished, and you were going to meet mine despite their reservations due to your wealth. Sydney!

But I can't bring myself to confess; all I can do is ask him to leave. "Please," I whisper this time, as I wrap my hands around my body, hoping to hold myself together from the outside. My heart, shattering inside, threatens to release all my emotions from the last ten years.

Without a word, he rises from the bed, the shuffling beside me indicating his departure. I watch as he collects his belongings, hurriedly dressing himself before striding toward the door.

"Shut the door on your way out," I instruct firmly, feeling tears welling up behind my closed eyelids.

Gabe steps out of the room, closing the door behind him and leaving me alone with the echoes of his presence. I find myself torn between the ache of his absence and the overwhelming need for solitude.

I am consumed by anger, gripped by fear. The memory of that fateful day in the hospital echoes in my mind, where I had begged for Gabe's presence, my screams expressing the agony coursing through my body.

It was supposed to be a good day, but I couldn't even appreciate it. Instead, I mourned the remains of a once-happy relationship with a man who had completely forgotten my entire existence.

CHAPTER 10

Sydney

The air smells of fresh grass and a tinge of dust, the feel of my soles meeting the grass mixed with the sound of rustling leaves and the neighing of the horses nearby.

After my emotional episode in my room, I made my way to the shower and washed away my anger. And slept deeply. When I awoke, for some reason, I had walked right out of the Hartwell mansion with an empty stomach and no clear destination in mind.

Now, here I am, standing in a stable, surrounded by unfamiliar faces tending to horses.

Inhaling deeply, I fill my lungs with the distinct smell of stable air, only to be overwhelmed by the offensive odor of feces. The unpleasant scent mirroring my equally foul mood and exacerbating my frustration. It's quite upsetting how the walk that was supposed to calm me down only aggravates me further.

My thoughts drift to Gabe far more often than I can count. I am painfully aware of how misguided and unfair it was to project my emotions onto Gabe as I did. Still, I had no ability to think rationally and limited time before I fell apart. I had to distance myself from him, and there was no way to explain my feelings to him then.

It felt like I was reliving something I had wanted Gabe to witness, and the bitter reality of his absence during my moments of desperation, contrasting with his current presence, stung deeply.

I have no idea how to proceed. I had finally accepted the reality of being Sara Jensen, Gabriel Hartwell's physical therapist, and nothing more. But last night's events have left my feelings all over the place.

Am I still in love with Gabriel Hartwell? It has been ten years, and in those long years, I have gotten married, had a son, and endured a stressful divorce. And, if Gabe ever gets his memory back, he won't be pleased to discover my ex-husband, the man I ended up marrying, had been his best friend. Gabe could never understand the depth of support Brad provided me during my most challenging moments and how it felt right to build a life with him at the time.

The hospital memory creeps into my mind, threatening to overthrow my current emotional balance as I walk. I shake it away, earning a few perplexed glances. Ignoring them, I peek at my phone's screen to check the time. Noon is fast approaching. I missed today's scheduled session. I am sure Gabe is upset. After all, I had practically thrown myself at him and slept with him, only to kick him out right afterward. Then I don't show up for my job that I'm actually here to do.

As I stand lost in my thoughts, contemplating the complexities of my situation, the sound of approaching footsteps interrupts the tranquility. I turn to see who it is, and to my surprise, it's Gabe.

He's wearing a slightly disheveled brown riding jacket that hugs his broad shoulders, accentuating his physique. Beneath the jacket, he wears a simple black polo shirt paired with well-worn riding pants. The dark brown riding breeches cling to his legs, perfectly molding to his powerful strides. He's waking naturally, without a cane, and apparently pain-free.

His usually meticulously styled wavy brown hair is slightly tousled, adding to the rawness of his appearance. However, his expression betrays his foul mood, evident in his furrowed brows and pursed lips. As he draws nearer, I can discern the unspoken questions lingering in his gaze, demanding an explanation for my actions. He clearly carries the weight of our unresolved situation just as heavily as I do. But I'm not mentally prepared to engage in conversation with him yet.

"Sara," he says curtly, his tone laced with frustration. Without giving me a chance to respond, he grabs my arm and leads me toward the back of the stables.

"Gabe, what are you doing?" I protest, attempting to pull away from his firm grip, my racing heartbeat trying to catch up with his sudden proximity and the dense tension between us.

The back of the stables is empty, except for a few scattered hay bales and horses' occasional rustling sound in their stalls. In a secluded corner of the wooden building, Gabe finally releases his grip and starts pacing.

"Look, Sara," he begins, his voice straining, "I want an explanation! Last night was..." His words trail off before evolving into a groan, his hands now tugging at the roots of his hair.

"Gabe, please try to calm down." I shift uncomfortably, my hands itching to reach out to him, but I'm not sure he would appreciate my touch. What exactly am I supposed to do now? He's agitated, and I'm the primary reason for his agitation.

He pauses, his pacing slowing as his gaze locks with mine, searching for answers. "I can't calm down, Sara," he replies, closing the space between us with a few steps.

"There's something undeniably familiar about you, and last night... it just felt right," he continues, his gaze soft yet penetrating, as if searching for confirmation in my eyes. "Wasn't it the same for you? I've wondered about that since you asked me to leave your room."

"It was!" I exclaim, unable to bear the thought of him thinking otherwise. It felt more than right, but I hold back the words.

A small smile plays on his lips as he reaches out, his fingers delicately tangling with the loose strands of my hair. "You have interesting ways of expressing your satisfaction, Miss Jensen. I just can't seem to figure you out," he whispers, leaning closer as he cups my face. My chest continues its incessant thrumming as I struggle to catch up with the sudden change in his tone.

"I can't seem to figure you out, either, Gabe. I didn't realize you would be so affected by my dismissal," I admit, glancing at his lips before refocusing on his eyes.

"I'm genuinely interested in you. I hope that's the only impression I'm leaving."

I swallow. He is? I'm taken aback by his words. The possibility of Gabe being interested in me hadn't crossed my mind before. Yesterday's events felt like fleeting moments; truth be told, I expected him to pretend it had never happened. But now, he's voicing his interest in me.

In Sara Jensen, not me. The thought shakes my reality. He is interested in me as the woman I am posing to be, as his physical therapist, not as Sydney. It feels wrong, but as I look at him, feeling the warmth of his skin, it's difficult to fully grasp the extent of the wrongness.

"You don't need to think about it, Sara. If you're not, it is perfectly all right, and we can continue our professionalism," he rambles on, removing his hand. It seems he took my silence as an adverse reaction to his confession.

I grab his jacket without thinking, fisting the cool material between my fingers, and pull him closer, meeting his lips with mine, hoping the action alone will convey everything I long to say.

Whether as Sara or as Sydney, I have been offered another chance with Gabe. While I know I will eventually have to reveal the truth, I decide to set aside that worry for now. At this moment, I simply want to revel in the knowledge that, even after all these years and without his memories, Gabe still recognizes a part of me, a part of us–our connection.

Gabe kisses me back with an intensity that shakes my knees as they weaken and threaten to give out. Luckily, he's holding me tight enough that I don't fall. It lasts a while with our lips locked in a gentle, passionate embrace, moving in sync, tugging at each other.

When I finally pull away, we're both panting heavily, breathing rapidly, smiling at each other as we let a moment of silence pass between us.

"I hope that clears up any doubts," I whisper, feeling my cheeks flush.

"It surpassed all my expectations," Gabe replies, his breath brushing against my face, his voice colored with a raspy undertone.

"By the way, what's with the outfit?" I ask, gesturing toward his disheveled brown riding jacket and snug riding pants.

He chuckles, running a hand through his slightly tousled hair. "I was on my way to the stables for a horse ride. It helps me relieve stress."

He used to play hockey to relieve stress, spend hours gracefully skating on ice, fervently shooting pucks into nets, or simply gliding with ease. Occasionally, I would accompany him, sitting on the sidelines, observing his skillful movements. However, it saddens me to acknowledge that he can't yet rediscover solace in playing hockey. His files revealed that his injury greatly restricts his mobility, rendering him incapacitated whenever he pushes himself too hard on the ice. It is disheartening to contemplate how something that once brought him peace has now become a source of distress. At least he's found a temporary replacement in riding.

The mention of the stables sparks my curiosity. "You found me here?" I inquire, glancing around the unfamiliar surroundings and the rustling trees.

Gabe nods, never breaking his gaze from mine. "Yes, I spotted you from a distance and felt compelled to come over. I needed to talk to you," he confesses.

A warmth spreads through me, realizing the significance of his presence. "You could have chosen to ignore what happened last night, but you sought me out instead," I remark, hoping he understands how much his gesture means to me.

He takes a step closer, closing the remaining distance between us. "Sara, I can't ignore the connection we share. It feels too real, too important," he admits.

A shy smile graces my lips as I contemplate his words. "Since we're here at the stables, how about we spend some time together? Maybe you can introduce me to the world of horse riding," I suggest, considering his earlier purpose and that we already missed his therapy session for the day.

Gabe's eyes light up with enthusiasm. "I'd love that," he eagerly replies. Despite being in his early-thirties, there are moments when he displays a charming innocence.

As we make our way to the stables, conversation flows effortlessly between us. My original plan had been to walk, exhaust myself with thoughts, and retreat to my room afterward.

I ponder the twist of fate that brought us together. If Gabe hadn't found me or had chosen to ignore last night's events, our dynamic as a physical therapist and client would have been marred by awkwardness and unspoken tension.

I imagine the discomfort that would have tainted our conversations, the constant undercurrent of unspoken words. The professional boundaries would have been strained, making it difficult to concentrate on his therapy without the weight of our shared secret hanging between us.

Instead, we are walking side by side, embarking on an adventure that holds the promise of discovery and a deeper connection. The stables, with their aroma of hay and the soothing sounds of horses, provide a tranquil backdrop to our unfolding journey.

The sight of the horses grazing and the sound of their hushed neighing welcomes us. As I look around, Gabe and I stand there, planted on dry hay.

"So, have you ever ridden a horse before, Sara?" Gabe inquires.

I chuckle nervously. "To be honest, Gabe, I've never had the opportunity. But I'm open to trying new experiences," I reply, hoping he can't hear the anxiety in my voice.

A smile curves on Gabe's lips. "It's okay to be nervous, but rest assured, you're in good hands."

I smile and think, *I know I am.*

CHAPTER 11

Gabriel

In the years gone by, or at least the ones that remain etched in my memory, I have traversed a multitude of sexual encounters with various women.

There were electrifying one-night stands and entanglements that lasted for months. I have navigated the realms of dating, but each time, the hollowness within me grew too heavy to sustain those connections, prompting me to sever ties to spare anyone further wasted time.

At some point, I concluded I had lost the ability to maintain a deep connection with someone, but Sara Jensen strikes my heart in ways I have never felt before.

But then again, I just might not remember that feeling.

Sara knows who I was before the accident. I am sure of it. Something happened between us that has her afraid to reveal whatever relationship we shared, and I will find out the truth.

"Take a moment to breathe before we start the next exercise," she says, her lips moving with mesmerizing grace, or maybe I'm simply imagining it.

Propelling myself through the water with effortless strokes, I move toward her, my legs fluttering gently beneath the surface until I wrap my arm around her slender waist. As I do, a subtle furrow forms on her brow, her eyes narrowing in an attempt to discern the intricacies of my thoughts. Sara's beauty is truly captivating, a vision to be cherished.

Her eyes sparkle with a captivating depth, the delicate curve of her petite nose accentuating her face, the tips of her ears, and her silky brown tresses. Every aspect of her being is utterly beautiful.

In a barely audible murmur, I utter, "Beautiful." The words escape my lips, tendrils of sound drifting toward her ears. Instantly, she turns her face, her lips poised between a smile that begs to emerge and the restraint she chooses to uphold.

"Mr. Hartwell, please refrain from flirting during your sessions. It's unprofessional," she playfully asserts, her palms placed on my chest in a gentle force to create a slight distance between us.

"What if I pay you to be unprofessional?" With that inquiry hanging in the air, I plant my lips on her chin.

Delightful laughter erupts from her lips. "I can consider the offer if you throw in a couple more of those kisses," she teases, her voice colored with a hint of playful seduction.

"Deal. Expect the money by this evening," I reply, a smirk tugging at the corners of my lips. "As for the kisses..." Without hesitation, I capture the velvety skin just above her collarbone, eliciting a sharp gasp.

Her voice caresses my name, "Gabe." The sound permeates through me, stirring a pulsating response within my body. Yet, I know it is crucial to pull away. The pool, after all, is not the appropriate setting to fulfill the desires I harbor for Sara.

Placing a tender kiss on her neck, I lean back, bringing my gaze to hers. "How about lunch today with me? In my study?" I propose, observing the delicate flutter of her eyelids as she contemplates my offer.

Sara shakes her head, the bridge of her brows creasing atop her nose. "And risk Hugh dropping in on you and me? I don't think so," she expresses firmly. "My room, sneak in. I'll prepare the food," she suggests.

Although sneaking around leaves me uneasy, I acknowledge the potential challenges she would face in maintaining her professional role as my physical therapist if our entanglement is brought to light. Besides, her presence in my home is a cherished delight that I am reluctant to relinquish.

I'm not ready to lose that yet.

With reluctance, I mutter, "All right then. I will happily sneak around in my home for you." The words slip from my lips, surprising both of us.

Deep down, however, I yearn to showcase my relationship with Sara openly. She deserves to be proudly displayed rather than concealed. Yet, amid our connection, one question looms large: Have we truly defined the nature of our relationship?

"Great. I'll see you at one o'clock," she responds, her voice resonating with warmth, as her lips brush against my cheek before she gracefully pivots away.

Emerging from the water, she hoists herself onto the glistening blue tiles, delicate droplets cascading from her swimwear and rolling down her supple form, leaving a trail of moisture in their wake.

I watch the rhythmic sway of her hips as she traverses the distance to the hallway, a sight that evokes certain explicit images within the recesses of my mind. Firmly, I shake my head, dismissing those thoughts, letting a smile overtake my lips.

As she vanishes into the corridor outside the pool area, I take a moment to collect myself, allowing the surge of anticipation to ebb away. It's time to resume the day, to immerse myself in the mundane tasks that await, and above all, to task my mother with delving into Sara's background.

There remains an abundance of unknowns about her, too much to ignore. My curiosity only intensifies with each passing day. In her subtle actions, Sara often hints at a familiarity with my habits, preferences, and idiosyncrasies. It is a peculiar connection, simultaneously alarming and comforting.

I make my way down the familiar path to my bedroom, taking the opportunity to freshen up and dress for the day ahead. With my lunch plans with Sara in mind, I deviate from my usual casual attire and opt for something more refined–a green patterned button-up shirt, accompanied by loose white pants and comfortable leather sandals.

Although our lunch will be an indoor affair, I believe dressing up for our little date is still appropriate. As I approach the door to her room, it swings open, revealing her silhouette draped in an oversized beige button-up shirt and matching lounge skirt. Her relaxed attire contrasts mine. Her hazel eyes gracefully traverse my appearance, examining me from head to toe, eliciting a delighted hum.

"Gabe, you look quite..." she begins, her voice trailing.

"Charming, handsome, dare I say, beautiful?" I interject playfully, watching as her features split into a breathtaking smile, brightening her face.

Her chest vibrates with laughter as she shakes her head lightly. "Come on in," she invites, turning on her heel and guiding me further into her room. I follow suit, gently guiding the black door to a close behind me.

An enchanting aroma fills the air, dominated by the tantalizing fragrance of strawberries with a subtle hint of orange. Shifting my focus, I discover the source–a white platter resting on the cream-colored sheets of her bed.

The plate of strawberry cheesecake immediately captures my attention. Despite my general inclination to avoid sweets, I have a particular fondness for strawberry cheesecake. It was a preference my mother had unveiled long ago, and I have always held a deep affinity for this delectable treat. A feeling in my gut tells me Sara is also aware of this fact, hence the presence of the cheesecake at our lunch.

Sara settles at the edge of her bed, perched beside the alluring platter. Her expectant gaze beckons me to join her, and I hesitate, slowly closing the door behind me. As it latches, I subtly flick the lock and step forward.

Her eyes follow me curiously, and I smile. "Dessert for lunch?"

"You've already had your workout for today. I thought it couldn't hurt."

It couldn't, she was right. "I worked harder than you, though, Miss Jensen."

When her lips part, I notice how her brows pull together in confusion. Does she think I'm insulting her?

I move to the bed, leaning down as my fingers wrap the back of her slender neck, my thumb running along her jaw to tip her head back so I can capture her lips.

Sara tastes like strawberries, and I groan softly as I steal the flavor for myself, my tongue brushing hers as I keep the kiss slow, stirring until I pull back.

My hands slide up her smooth, bare thighs, pushing up her skirt to her hips as our eyes meet, and that furrow of confusion disappears.

"Gabe..." The tone must have been aimed at chiding, but I tip her back onto the bed, the forks rattling on the tray, and she laughs. "Gabe, we can't!"

"I'm hungry," I grin, dipping my head down to graze the inside of her thigh with my lips. Her answering gasp tells me she understands fully now, and her hips squirm as I lower to my knees, ignoring the twinge of pain.

Her sweet scent tickles my brain—a light, fragrant soap that makes my mouth water. I kiss up the inside of her thigh, then lift her leg to drape it over my shoulder. I can feel her tense with anticipation as my lips move to where her thigh and hip meet so my teeth can grip the silken fabric of her panties, tugging them down slowly.

Her natural scent makes my head swim with its intoxicating familiarity, and all of my blood goes straight to my cock as it strains against my pants.

I wanted to take it slow, but my brain clicks off. Something else grabs ahold of me as I lean in, dragging the flat of my tongue over her slit, the fingers of my left hand tugging her panties down to her knees.

"Gabe!" she cries out for me, and it fuels me as I straighten my tongue and flick it between her netherlips now, catching her clit with the tip. Her fingers immediately tangle in my hair, and I'm unsure if she will push me away or pull me closer, then she answers that thought as her instincts tug me closer.

I delve my tongue inside of her, wriggling it, and her hips squirm wildly in my grip. Her hand claps over her mouth to stifle her cries as I flick it in and out of her.

I want more. I want her writhing. My left hand joins in as I move my tongue's attention to her clit and press my middle and ring finger inside of her.

Her hand moves out to the side, grabbing her pillow, and when she stuffs it over her face to muffle herself further, I chuckle despite myself. She's so sexy and so cute all at once; it's almost overwhelming to me, so I decide to overwhelm her myself. The need for retribution for these feelings rises inside me.

I pump my hand in tandem with closing my lips around her clit, suckling, flicking my tongue, enjoying the sting of the way she pulls my hair, the way she struggles not to close her thighs.

Her muffled cries are wordless, but they're all for me, and an odd possessive flame flickers to life inside of me, growing hotter with each sound.

Her walls squeeze my fingers, and I let go of her leg to push down on her upper abdomen to increase the pressure.

"Shh, shh, shh," I tease her while her back arches off the bed. "A little more." And then I give her everything I have, hitting that bundle of nerves inside of her, setting my oral muscle to work overtime as I groan against her.

When she finishes, I'm mad for the taste of her, letting my tongue drag slowly, my heartbeat pounding in my ears, barely letting in the sounds of her ragged, pleasured breaths.

I wait, letting her come down from the high, then fix her panties and skirt. When she moves the pillow to look at me with that flushed face, I grin.

Standing up proves a bit more difficult than I'd like, but I manage, and head to her bathroom, giving her a moment to compose herself. When I return, her cheeks are still flushed, but she's dressed as she was when I walked in.

I had a thought while I was cleaning up. I wanted to know her, know more, let my knowledge match these bizarre feelings in me.

As I settle beside Sara on the bed, my gaze shifts from the delectable spread of food to her face tilted downward. "Sara," I call, and she hums in response, her fingers reaching for a butter knife at the edge of the platter.

"Tell me about your life outside of our sessions. Tell me about your son," I casually demand, keeping my focus on her.

There is a subtle shift in her body language, an awkwardness that emanates from her as she hesitates before finally turning her eyes to meet mine. A flicker of uncertainty dances in Sara's hazel eyes, her brows knitting together ever so slightly. She seems caught off guard by my demand, her fingers momentarily freezing in their pursuit of the butter knife. I watch intently as a conflicted expression crosses her features, her lips parting slightly as if searching for the right words.

Her hand, hovering hesitantly above the knife, eventually lowers to rest on her lap. With a deep breath, Sara begins to speak. "Just like Katie is to you... Damon is my world," she starts. "He's ten years old and has been the sole reason I've been holding on for quite some time now." As she speaks, her gaze seems to drift off into the distance, her fingers absentmindedly tracing invisible patterns on her thigh. "I would like to talk about him with you, I would, but..." she pauses.

Sara's unease was palpable, her body language betraying her attempt to hide her discomfort. The room seems to grow quieter as her silence stretches, punctuated only by the faint sound of her shallow breaths.

After a moment of contemplation, she meets my gaze once more. "I... I can't share much about him," she admits softly, her voice laced with a hint of something imperceivable. "It's complicated."

Curiosity tugs at me, a longing to understand the woman beside me, but I know I have to let it be until she is more comfortable sharing that part of herself with me.

"And your ex-husband?" I inquire gently, refusing to acknowledge the bitter taste of the word "ex-husband" in my mouth.

Sara's lips curve into a melancholic smile, her eyes shimmering with unspoken pain. "We divorced two years ago," she reveals. "He had... ugh, someone else, you see." Her words hang in the air, pregnant with the weight of betrayal.

I observe Sara closely, taking in the subtle shifts in her expressions as she shares these intimate details. Her eyes, clouded earlier with sorrow, now sparkle with resilient strength. Her voice has a vulnerability, a raw honesty that resonates deeply within me.

"He had a mistress on the side," she continues, her voice steadier than before. "And it took me a while to gather the strength to walk away. But I eventually did, for myself and Damon."

The air seems to thicken with unspoken emotions as Sara's story unfolds. I can sense the layers of pain and growth she experienced, the resilience that has shaped her into the woman sitting beside me.

Sara's smile widens, transforming into one of quiet triumph. "But enough about the past," she says, her voice colored with newfound enthusiasm. "Let me tell you something about myself. I adore running. It's my escape. I used to run track from high school into college."

Sara's eyes light up as she speaks, pushing aside the heaviness of her earlier revelations. The vulnerability in her voice has shifted into quiet confidence, as if sharing this part of herself is bringing her a sense of liberation.

Although Sara has divulged a wealth of information about herself, a nagging thought tugs at the corners of my mind, reminding me that our searches before hiring her had yielded no information suggesting that Sara Jensen had been married or had any children that could distract her from her work as my physical therapist. Those aspects stood out prominently among the myriad factors contributing to her strong candidacy for the job.

While I hesitate to cast doubt upon Sara, I can't help but feel a pang of curiosity. I yearn to unravel the enigma of her concealed personal life and discover whose hands I entrust my heart to.

I decide to seek assistance from my mother. I will request she conduct a thorough background check on Sara Jensen, extending beyond her association with PTX, the company she works for. Regardless of the nature of the matter, I aim to find the truth. I will deal with any consequences later on, should they arise.

CHAPTER 12

Sydney

I have consciously avoided addressing the lingering thought, telling myself I will confront it later. Yet, the truth remains. I can't dismiss it entirely. It persistently resurfaces no matter how hard I try to push it aside while in Gabe's company.

Sara Jensen—I am *not* Sara Jensen. Sara Jensen is merely a name I am not entitled to, but Gabe believes otherwise. Our relationship has been steadily progressing, inching closer to the inevitable moment he will uncover the truth.

What if he perceives it as a deliberate deception? The thought of Gabe misunderstanding my intentions and pushing me away, the thought of losing him once again is unsettling.

Each fleeting moment we manage to steal away within the confines of the Hartwell mansion only serves to amplify the unresolved emotions I harbor for him. They have become catalysts, intensifying my feelings with his mere presence.

Sooner or later, I will have to tell him who I am: Sydney Pearce, his former fiancée, a forgotten figure in his memory. I long for him to say my name once again.

I turn a corner to Gabe's study, only to encounter a silhouette obstructing my path. It is Larissa Hartwell, of all people. A wave of surprise and fear washes over me at her sudden presence.

She stands at the corner's edge, her movements momentarily frozen. Clad in a black day dress adorned with a silver brooch gracing her left breast, she emanates an air of poise.

"Miss Jensen, quite a coincidence running into you here. I was headed your way," she remarks in a monotone voice, her expression devoid of any amusement. Her narrowed brown eyes bore into mine, a sense of familiarity accompanying her gaze.

Swallowing the lump at the back of my throat, I feel my heartbeat quicken, straying from its regular rhythm. Something feels amiss. Why would Larissa Hartwell actively seek me out? Has she found out about Gabe and me? No, that seems highly unlikely. We have been exceedingly cautious in our endeavors. Has she discovered the source of my familiarity?

"Oh, Mrs. Hartwell. To what do I owe the pleasure of this visit?" I inquire nonchalantly, carefully veiling any traces of anxiety in my tone. I shouldn't let her sense my nervousness.

"Well," she begins, pausing briefly as she purses her lips, an almost imperceptible gesture. "Let us discuss this matter in a more private setting," the older lady urges, stepping past me as she speaks.

I follow in her wake, each step sending a chill through my body, leaving me with an unsettling coldness. I want to be anywhere other than here with Larissa Hartwell.

We proceed along a path leading to an unfamiliar section of the Hartwell mansion, passing corridors that bypass my bedroom and the bustling kitchen. I can't shake the growing suspicion that Larissa intends to lead me to some secluded spot, away from prying eyes, to possibly end my life.

I'm not sure I would put it past her, considering all the terrible things she has said to me in the past. She continues her confident stride, with me trailing behind until, at last, we arrive at a secluded corridor that seems to lead to a storage area.

"Much better," she remarks, lightly tapping the fabric of her dress as if brushing away any imaginary specks of dirt. "Now, can you please explain yourself?" she demands icily, her words laced with hostility–a tone I had encountered numerous times as Sydney Pearce.

It hits me like a wall of ice. Larissa has discovered my true identity.

My heartbeat rams against my chest with violence, my breath uneven as it rushes in and out of my lungs rapidly. I clench my arm behind my back, digging my nails into my own flesh in an attempt to regain my composure.

There is no denying it. All I can focus on now is minimizing the fallout and containing the damage. Larissa Hartwell possesses the power to ruin me with a mere flick of her wrist, and if I'm not cautious, I stand to lose far more than just Gabe's trust.

"I saw an opportunity, and I simply took it," I admit truthfully. "Sara wasn't around, and I posed as her to meet my client," I added, keeping my explanation concise. There is no need to beat around the bush. We are both grown women.

"Did you know Gabriel was your client?" she inquires, studying me intently with narrowed eyes.

"No. I found out upon my arrival," I reply curtly.

She hums in response, turning on her heel and taking a few measured steps, the impact of her soles on the concrete seemingly louder than they should be, before returning to her previous position.

"Well, then. What's done is done, but surely you must understand. I can't risk the both of you rekindling your joke of a relationship," she scoffs, letting out a hearty and wicked laugh at the thought.

My nails dig into my skin, and I feel a stinging sensation. I bite back the spiteful words that dance on the tip of my tongue, recognizing that I am in no position to allow emotions to guide my actions.

Assuming someone else's identity and accepting a contract under false pretenses meant facing dire consequences if authorities become involved. I was well aware of the risks, yet I had never anticipated this particular turn of events. Perhaps my confidence in my abilities had been misguided, and my leniency in maintaining my disguise had been a grave mistake.

Or I should have simply never let my desperation push me into it. However, there is no use in dwelling on it now. I need to ensure PTX and I emerge from this situation unscathed.

The pressing question now is: what will Larissa Hartwell do with this information?

"What do you want from me?" I interject, getting straight to the point and gradually releasing my grip on my arm.

"Leave, and don't tell anyone. I won't, either. Having you arrested would raise suspicions from Gabriel, and if he discovers your true identity, there's a chance his memories might resurface, and I cannot allow that," she approaches me, narrowing the gap between us. "I simply cannot have you enter my son's life again. You would only serve as a distraction. Blake was to be the next CEO of Hartwell Enterprises but now Gabe must take on that role."

Her words cut deep, evoking a torrent of tears that well up within my eyes. I blink quickly, attempting to bat them away.

"And just to show my generosity, seeing as you did help him make significant progress, the contract will remain intact. The Hartwells will fund PTX and its expansion. You will never lay eyes on my son again," she spits bitterly. "My associates will send you the necessary documents. I never want to see you again, Sydney Pearce," she declares before brushing past me and striding away.

I collapse to my knees, clutching the fabric of my blouse tightly against my chest. What does this mean for Gabe and me? What do I do now? Larissa has made her threats abundantly clear, and she is even offering to fund PTX, just as I had always wanted.

I am not getting arrested, and I am securing the funding for the clinic, but at the cost of losing Gabe again.

I am no longer a carefree twenty-year-old who can make decisions solely for herself. I have a family to care for, a son who depends on me. I can't fulfill those responsibilities from the confines of a jail cell or without the necessary resources.

However, as a woman and a lover, my heart still yearns for Gabe. The mere thought of parting ways with him, of being separated from him once more, is absolutely anguishing.

With tears streaming down my face, I slowly rise from the cold, unforgiving floor. The weight of Larissa's ultimatum settles heavily on my shoulders, reminding me of the difficult choice I have to make. Staying at the Hartwell mansion will only lead to heartache and further complications.

I have to leave Gabe.

As I retrace my steps, each corridor seems longer and narrower than before, as if they are trying to hold me back. Little bits of memories with Gabe flood my mind, overlapping with the reality unraveling before me. The stolen moments, the whispered promises, and the passionate kisses—they all seem like fragile dreams, slipping away with each passing second.

Reaching my bedroom, I push open the door with trembling hands. The room feels different now, its walls echoing with the memories we created. I can't bear to think about any of them. I have to act swiftly, lest I lose my resolve.

A sense of urgency surges through me, and I move with purpose. I open the drawers and cabinets, hastily gathering my belongings. The soft touch of fabric, the weight of trinkets, his scent lingering on the sheets–I try not to let them distract me from the task at hand.

I stuff clothes, toiletries, and personal items into the waiting suitcases, my actions becoming increasingly frantic. The room itself seems to understand the urgency as if it is trying to help me. The bed creaks in quiet encouragement, urging me to hasten my pace.

Just as I finish zipping up the last suitcase, a sharp knock resonates through the room, jolting me from my desperate focus. My heart races, and I freeze in place, the sound reverberating in my ears. Who could it be? Is it Larissa? Did she change her mind?

Taking a deep breath, I glance around the room for signs of my hasty departure. I quickly drag the still-open suitcases under the large four-poster bed, concealing them from view.

The knocking persists, growing impatient. My hands continue to tremble as I smooth down my disheveled hair, desperately trying to compose myself. It is crucial to maintain the facade, to not give away my anxiousness.

At that moment, a heaviness settles in my chest, and I silently vow that this won't be the end. No matter the distance or the circumstances, I will find a way back to Gabe, even if just to explain myself. He deserves that much.

With a deep breath, I open the door to find Larissa Hartwell herself outside my door. "I trust you're getting ready," she states in a level tone.

I suppress the urge to scoff loudly, even though her eagerness to get rid of me is palpable. Maintaining my composure, I simply nod, swallowing my pride.

"Marvelous," she declares, her tone brimming with satisfaction. "You will depart at the crack of dawn tomorrow morning. I have arranged your transportation."

With her words, the stark reality of my imminent departure fully sinks in. The gravity of the situation is undeniable, and I realize that this is not a mere transition but a definitive departure from the familiar.

I am leaving the Hartwell mansion. I am leaving Gabe.

CHAPTER 13

Sydney

A sharp knock cuts through my daydreaming in the peace of my office, making me jump.

"Miss Pearce, the Hartwells have sent over a parcel." Jane's voice reverberates through the walls as she opens the door slightly, her head appearing in the crack of the doorway.

"Please, come in," I beckon, my voice emerging dry and hoarse.

Jane enters the room. With each deliberate stride, the sound of her heels resonates against the floor, gradually approaching my desk, where she gingerly places the large yellow envelope on the polished mahogany.

"Thank you, Jane," I express my gratitude, to which she simply nods, turns, and confidently strides back out of my office.

Retrieving my reading glasses, I delicately position them on my face, preparing myself for the task at hand. With anticipation, I run my fingers along the surface of the vibrant yellow parcel, feeling its texture under my touch. Slowly, I pull it open to reveal a meticulously organized folder containing a large collection of papers.

I scrutinize the file's contents with utmost care, methodically reading every word, dissecting each clause, and examining every sentence. Larissa has faithfully upheld her promise. She has agreed to provide the necessary funding for PTX. All that remains is adding my signature to the documents and returning them to her.

Gently placing the papers back into a stack on my desk, I remove my glasses, feeling a slight relief to the bridge of my nose as I instinctively massage the area, soothing the discomfort from the frames.

Just two days have passed since leaving the mansion, and still no word from Gabe. I am certain that Larissa is employing every possible means to hinder our communication, just as she did ten years ago. The prospect of her doing so again looms over me, casting a shadow of uncertainty. What has she told him about me?

What should I do? I had resolved myself before, sure of my decision to take this opportunity as the right choice, but now that I'm here, now that the documents are staring up at me, I can't bring myself to sign them.

Although the act of signing this document can potentially exacerbate the current misunderstandings between me and Gabe, I can't ignore the fact that my future and my son's future hinges on this opportunity. The magnitude of the situation is overwhelming. The prospect of taking a well-deserved respite from work crosses my mind. Since returning to the office, I haven't allowed myself the luxury of a break. I have been tirelessly attempting to make up for the neglected aspects of my life and the company, including my pursuit of Sara Jensen.

I have not received any communication from her thus far. If necessary, I am determined to take legal action against her for neglecting her duties and breach of contract.

Feeling the weight of the decision pressing too heavily upon me, I decide to visit my son. Pushing my chair back, I stand up from my desk, leaving the meticulously organized folder behind. As I walk toward the office door, the gravity of the situation slowly fades from my mind, and my thoughts drift toward Damon.

Leaving the confines of my office, I step into the hallway, greeted by the soft glow of the ambient lighting. The familiar scent of polished wood and fresh flowers fills the air, momentarily easing my troubled thoughts.

With deliberate strides, I make my journey toward the entrance with purpose, distancing myself from my responsibilities and the heavy decisions waiting for me.

Exiting the building, I am met with the bustling cityscape before me. The honking of car horns, the measured footsteps of San Diego's pedestrians, and the distant hum of life envelops my senses. Raising my hand, I hail a passing yellow cab, its vibrant color almost matching the brightness of the hot sun.

As the taxi approaches the curb, I notice its arrival and swiftly open the door before gracefully sliding into the backseat. The worn leather seat welcomes me, offering a momentary respite from the chaos outside. With a deep breath, I instruct the driver to take me to my ex-husband's apartment.

Damon has been staying with Brad and has reached the point where it is appropriate for me to bring him back to my place. As my workload gradually lessens, the timing seems reasonable for this transition.

As we navigate through the city streets, I find my thoughts drifting to memories of Brad. He and I had once been just friends, then lovers, and now an irrevocable circumstance has driven a wedge between us.

It has been two years since I divorced him, and the remnants of our failed marriage still haunt me, albeit in a transformed state. Upon reflection, it became evident that the signs were present from the very outset. Our union was never based on love, at least not from my perspective.

The cab comes to a halt outside Brad's apartment building. I pay the fare, thanking the lively old driver before stepping onto the sidewalk. Taking a moment to collect myself, I navigate the familiar surroundings, ascending the small steps before reaching the entrance.

I press the buzzer harshly and wait for a response, shooting glances at the buildings around me. After a brief yet seemingly endless wait, the door finally yields, emitting a faint click that signifies my access has been granted. Climbing the stairs, I reach his apartment door and raise my hand, hesitating briefly before knocking softly.

The door swings open almost immediately, revealing Damon, who greets me with a broad smile stretching across his face. His eyes, a captivating shade of hazel, glisten under the artificial lighting of the apartment. Without hesitation, he rushes into my embrace, enfolding me in a tight, heartfelt hug. The warmth of his presence envelops me, momentarily easing the weight of my worries.

"Mom!" Damon's voice is full of genuine joy. "I missed you so much!"

All the worries plaguing me throughout the past week suddenly vanish, giving way to a wave of affection for my son. Softly, I murmur, "I missed you too, sweetie." With an eager smile, I continue, "Go get your things. We're going back home together."

"You won't stay a minute? Maybe have lunch together?" Brad's throaty voice carries toward me as he emerges into view.

He stands before me, clad in casual attire that accentuates his rugged charm. His blonde hair, tousled and carefree, frames his face and the familiar features I had come to know so well. His intense blue eyes gaze at me, accompanied by a disarming smile that had once held the power to reassure me during my toughest moments.

Despite his physical appeal, I know better than to let his charm sway me. He has a way of making me feel guilty for divorcing him, even though it was his infidelity that had shattered our marriage. I have to remind myself to remain firm and not allow his attempts at flirtation to penetrate my resolve.

"Hey," I greet him, maintaining a composed demeanor. "I appreciate the invitation, but today, I'm here to take Damon back home with me."

Brad's smile falls for a second, a flicker of disappointment creasing his features. However, he quickly replants a smile on his face as he leans against the doorway, his soft gaze fixed on me.

"You know, Sydney, we could give it another shot. I still love you, and maybe things could be different this time," he suggests, his voice colored by a tinge of hope.

He must be joking. I am aware I never harbored deep feelings for him, but I played my duties as a wife regardless. I was faithful. I sigh softly and step closer, meeting his gaze with a determined expression.

"Look, we've been down that road before," I reply. "It didn't work out, and I really do care about you, I do, but I can't bring myself to trust you again."

His face falls again, a flicker of hurt crossing his ocean eyes. He straightens up, pushing himself off the door frame before stepping toward me. His voice softens. "I understand. I just...

I miss what we had. But if you're happy now, that's what matters," he admits.

I nod, appreciating his understanding and the acknowledgment of my happiness. Damon's hurried footsteps approach.

"I have finished packing," he declares with enthusiasm while tugging his compact gray suitcase behind him.

"I am happy, Brad. I want you to be happy, too," I say sincerely. "But it's best to focus on co-parenting Damon and creating a positive environment for him. Our romantic relationship is in the past."

I approach Damon and extend my hand to retrieve his suitcase. As I do so, I playfully tousle his dark hair, eliciting a smile that adorns his lips. "Stop, you're messing up my hair," he jokingly protests.

We walk purposefully toward the entrance, where my ex-husband stands waiting. His gaze lands on me momentarily, his blue eyes searching for something he won't find. Suddenly, he nods.

"You're right, Sydney," he says, lowering his gaze to Damon. "Damon deserves the best from both of us."

With a final glance, I turn away from him, gently guiding Damon toward the stairs. As Damon and I descend the stairs, the weight of the moment lingers in the air.

We walk side by side, our footsteps creating a synchronized rhythm on the concrete steps. Damon's voice fills the space as he excitedly chats about his recent adventures with Brad and the games they have played.

I listen attentively, soaking in his words and their sheer innocence. Despite the complexities of my own life, there is solace in the simplicity of his tales. His voice echoes with pure joy, reminding me of the importance of nurturing his happiness.

As we reach the bottom of the staircase, the city unfolds before us once again. I raise my hand, hailing a passing yellow cab. Its tires screech as it comes to a stop at the curb, and I open the door, motioning for Damon to climb in first.

"Careful now," I say, offering a supportive hand as he settles into the backseat. I follow suit once he is comfortably seated, closing the door behind me. The worn leather seat greets me once more, its familiarity a small comfort amid the uncertainties of my current situation.

I exchange eye contact with the cab driver, a middle-aged man offering a small smile. "Could you please take us to 532 Wooten Avenue?" I request. The man nods gently, and with a swift movement, he maneuvers the vehicle back into the flow of traffic.

Damon's voice fills the cab as we navigate through the city, his words intermingling with the sounds outside. He chatters about his school friends, and I listen intently, occasionally interjecting.

Talking to him, I feel my priorities aligning, desperately calling my attention to the forefront of my mind. I can't delay making a decision any longer. The papers from Larissa's parcel remain on my desk, awaiting my signature, signifying my commitment to PTX and the future it holds for my family.

I look at Damon, his eyes gleaming with youthful innocence, and realize that my actions are not only about my own ambitions but also about creating a stable foundation for him. As a mother, I have a responsibility to provide him with a secure and nurturing environment, and the PTX expansion presents an opportunity to fulfill that duty.

And I plan on doing just that.

CHAPTER 14

Gabriel

"What do you mean you fired her?" The words, directed at my mother, leave my mouth echoing audibly around the drawing room, further increasing the tension.

I have made a horrible mistake.

"Gabriel, you specifically requested me to conduct a background check on her, and I carried out your request," my mother responds calmly, her composed demeanor only further aggravating me.

How could investigating Sara's past lead to her termination without my knowledge? The two actions have no apparent link.

"Precisely, not only have you not reported anything back to me, you've also decided to fire my physical therapist without my knowledge... the only one who I've made any significant progress with in over a year." I turn on my heel, frustration bubbling in my gut, threatening to explode in a release of anger.

This situation is not what I had anticipated. My intention was merely to gather more information about Sara, expecting the consequence to be her anger over being investigated, not my mother's unilateral decision to terminate her employment.

And now, here I stand in my swimwear, in the middle of my mother's drawing room, completely clueless about Sara's whereabouts or her emotional state. She must be aware that my mother initiated the background check on my behalf, and the pain she must be experiencing is unimaginable.

"Gabriel, I must admit, I find your agitation rather perplexing. After all, the person in question was merely a therapist–an easily replaceable professional."

"Easily replaceable? After almost ten years of therapy, she's made the most progress! Because of her I just might be able to resume full training."

It is no surprise that she doesn't understand. My mother and I seldom see eye to eye, as our personalities are starkly contrasting. Hence, I've never held many expectations for her understanding of my personal feelings.

Seeing little point in continuing the discussion, I storm out of the room, my mind set on a singular objective: finding Sara. And PTX serves as my initial destination.

As I stomp down the corridor, the tiles beneath my feet amplifying the impact of my agitated steps.

Reaching my bedroom, I swing open the door with an exasperated force, the hinges creaking in protest. My eyes scan the room, landing on the neatly folded garments laid out on the bed. A plain white towel, fresh and untouched, accompanied a set of dark clothing: a pair of black tailored trousers and a crisp white button-down shirt.

Stripping out of my swimwear impatiently, I dry my body with the towel, the fabric absorbing the pool water still clinging to my skin. I swiftly slip into the clean clothes without bothering to shower.

Once dressed, I spare a glance in the mirror, adjusting my collar with a flick of my fingers. The reflection staring back at me is that of a man with determination etched into his features, his jaw set, and his green eyes ablaze with purpose. With a final nod of affirmation to my reflection, I leave the room behind, focusing on my destination, PTX.

Navigating through the sprawling mansion and the opulent halls, I soon arrive at the entrance to the garages. As the automatic doors slide open, revealing many sleek, high-end vehicles, I hesitate momentarily, contemplating which one best suits my purpose. My gaze roves over the collection of automobiles, each a testament to my family's wealth and status. Eventually, my eyes settle on a midnight blue sports car, its lines exuding both power and elegance.

I locate the right key. Approaching the vehicle, I run my hand along its smooth surface, feeling the cool metal beneath my fingertips. With a decisive motion, I open the driver's door and settle into the supple leather seat. The engine purrs to life, a symphony of mechanical prowess.

As I pull out of the garage, the grand gates of the Hartwell estate loom before me, opening to grant me passage. The world beyond awaits, and I grip the steering wheel tightly, ready to face whatever obstacles lay ahead in my quest to find Sara.

As I merge into the flow of traffic, the bustling streets of San Diego stretch out before me. The rhythmic hum of the engine accompanies my racing thoughts, the car gliding through the urban landscape with ease. The car's GPS guides me toward PTX, Sara's workplace.

Driving through the streets, I ponder my newfound situation with Sara. How will I explain to Sara the reason behind my investigation? Will she understand? Or will she feel betrayed, believing that I violated her privacy?

In truth, my decision to delve into her past was driven by simple curiosity. Sara had entered my life unexpectedly, injecting it with a vitality I had long been missing. Her presence had become an important part of my daily routine, and I simply wanted to ensure I could trust her. That there were no hidden secrets that could jeopardize what was growing between us.

But my actions had backfired, resulting in her termination and undoubtedly causing her pain. I curse myself for not considering the consequences more thoroughly, and for not discussing my concerns with her directly. My mother's meddling has only exacerbated the situation, adding a layer of complexity that I now have to unravel.

As I maneuver through the city, the towering buildings and bustling pedestrians become a blur. The weight of my actions settles heavily on my shoulders, and I rehearse the words I will use to explain myself to Sara. I need her to understand that my intentions had been rooted in a desire for trust and security, even if my methods had been misguided.

Will she accept my apology? Will she be open to giving me another chance? I hope our connection, the bond we have formed, will be strong enough to weather this storm. I miss her so much.

It seems as though my mother had orchestrated the entire situation, deliberately choosing the evening when I received an urgent office summons that required me to leave the state. Unfortunately, I had to travel without informing Sara in advance. The circumstances were rather puzzling since in all the time we spent together, I never thought to ask for her contact information, leaving me unable to reach her all week. Though, I assumed she was informed of my trip and would be there when I returned.

Finally, the GPS indicates my arrival at PTX. I carefully maneuver the car into a parking spot and emerge onto the vibrant, sun-kissed street. PTX's sleek exterior looms in front of me, and almost immediately, a ringing sound pierces through my thoughts.

A cold sensation washes over me, and the ringing persists in my head, telling me I have been here before.

Sara's laughter echoes through my memory, but something about her appearance seems different as if she has turned back the clock and looks younger.

Her eyes gleam with excitement as she gazes at the building before us. "Okay, just imagine if I were to have a rehabilitation center right here," she exclaims with enthusiasm. "It would be absolutely fantastic."

"Here? Well, I suppose the location isn't all that bad, although it certainly needs significant renovations," I find myself blurting out, even though I hadn't meant to speak aloud.

"Of course! Do you honestly think I would leave that ghastly shade of brown untouched?" Sara cleverly retorts, her fingers gently grazing the wall's surface.

I chuckle in response to her remark, stepping closer and pulling her into an embrace. "Regardless of the color, I do not doubt that you will work wonders with this place, Sydney," I say sincerely, planting a tender kiss on her lips.

Sydney? The name escaped from my lips unconsciously, and it was as if the sound reverberated within the depths of my mind. Suddenly, I am jolted into another memory.

I'm driving past the building once again, yearning for Sydney's presence beside me to witness my departure. Her opposition to my decision to leave her here to attend the benefit alone with Blake and Ella was strong and unwavering. She is angry with me, almost unreasonably so, and not willing to meet with me before I leave. Despite my deep desire to stay and fulfill her wishes, I found myself unable to do so. My mother had explicitly commanded my attendance and I had been unable to convince her otherwise. All I wished for was Sydney's understanding.

Sydney? The name echoes in my thoughts again, the familiarity tugging at my mind aggressively.

As my vision blurs, the world around me gradually loses its clarity, morphing into an indistinct tableau before my eyes, and weariness takes over me. I struggle valiantly to maintain my balance, desperately clinging to my upright stance, but it becomes increasingly apparent that my strength is waning.

Overwhelmed by the burden of my weight, I yield to gravity, surrendering myself to the ground with a groaning collapse. My body is in disarray as I slump into a disheveled heap while my hands instinctively cradle my throbbing head in a feeble attempt to alleviate the pain. The last fragmented observation is the sight of a growing multitude of feet encircling me as I fade to blackness.

A peculiar soundscape envelops me. Faint beeps and electronic whirs permeate the air, accompanied by distant voices engaging in hushed conversations. The sounds seem to ebb and flow, like waves crashing against the shore of my fading awareness.

Amid the auditory haze, a persistent, rhythmic pulsation gradually grows louder. It starts as a subtle throb, like a drumbeat echoing in the distance, barely perceptible. But as the beat intensifies, it transforms into a dull, persistent pounding that reverberates through my skull. With each thump, my headache tightens its grip, its presence becoming increasingly undeniable.

My consciousness teeters on the precipice of awakening, the pain in my head serving as an anchor to this reality. Slowly, the fragmented pieces of memory begin to align, forming a tapestry of recollections that floods my mind. Once hazy and disoriented, the images now take shape with vivid clarity.

Sara. The drawing room. The confrontation with my mother. The abrupt termination of Sara's employment. The urgency of finding her. The drive through San Diego's streets. The anticipation of reaching PTX. The memories surge forward as if trying to provide an explanation for my current situation.

As my consciousness flutters closer to the surface, the sounds around me sharpen, taking on distinct tones and patterns. I can discern the measured footsteps of people scurrying around me, the soft murmurs of conversations being held just beyond my reach.

And then, a voice, gentle and reassuring, cuts through the auditory tapestry, seeping into my fragmented consciousness. "He's waking up," it announces, accompanied by the distant rustle of a coat.

My eyelids flutter, struggling against the bright lights pressing them shut. Gradually, the veil of darkness lifts, revealing a hospital room's sterile, fluorescent-lit surroundings. The subtle headache persists, throbbing in rhythm with the rapid fluttering of my awakening consciousness.

With a weary effort, I push myself up, wincing at the soreness that radiates through my body. As my vision focuses, I take in the sterile white walls, the medical equipment stationed by my bedside, and the concerned faces of doctors and nurses who have gathered around me.

Sudden awareness floods through me, washing away the remnants of confusion. I remember the events leading up to this moment–no longer limited to the past ten years.

My memories dance before my eyes, intertwining with the ache in my head, forming a portrait of tangled emotions and unanswered questions.

The foremost question that arose was: Why did Sydney Pearce, my fiancée, assume the identity of Sara Jensen?

CHAPTER 15

Gabriel

Moments ago, or what feels like moments ago, I was gripped with worry that my lack of communication with Sara over the few days may have inflicted irreparable damage upon our relationship. Now, I am painfully aware of the damage that has already been inflicted along the very seams that once held us together. Damage that I must now strive to rectify. Sydney, the love of my life, has likely endured these past years believing, falsely, that I abandoned her.

The mere thought of the hardships she must have faced during that time weighs heavily upon my heart. There must have been moments when she waited, hopeful for my return, only to be ultimately forced to move on from our relationship. Her son's existence now serves as undeniable proof that she had indeed moved forward. With a heavy swallow, I taste the bitterness of my situation, the anguish of all the moments I missed in her life.

However, she has rediscovered me as Sara Jensen, and once again, I have fallen deeply in love with her. We had something going on before my mother's intervention. It suddenly made sense why my mother fired her. She had recognized her during the background check I requested.

I long for Sydney. The ache of her absence is a constant reminder of our recent misunderstanding. It seems only yesterday when our voices clashed in a heated exchange over my last-minute decision to accompany my brother and sister-in-law to Los Angeles to support a Hartwell sponsored benefit gala alone, a choice made solely to placate my mother.

The past still hangs heavily upon me, as if time has stood still since the tragic day when my car collided with a truck. In that fateful moment, not only did I lose my beloved brother and his wife, but the wreckage also claimed the fragments of my own dreams—the shattered remnants of my once-promising hockey career, along with the damage inflicted upon my knees and my future with Sydney.

I should have stayed with her. Had I done so, I might have avoided all that heartache. The crash, the loss of life, my dreams, my memories—that decision changed everything.

A male doctor enters the room with confident strides, the customary white coat symbolizing his authority. "Mr. Hartwell," he begins, his voice maintaining a calm demeanor yet tinged with genuine concern. "After conducting more tests, I must inform you that you have sustained another concussion as a direct consequence of your latest fall. From your records, including your hockey career, that totals five concussions."

His words strike me with a disconcerting force. Another concussion? The revelation unsettles me, my mind trying to grasp the full implications.

The doctor continues, his explanation peppered with medical terminology meant to emphasize my condition's gravity. He describes the impact of the concussions on my brain, highlighting potential consequences such as memory loss, confusion, and difficulty concentrating. Each sentence he utters seems to magnify the weight of my predicament.

Ironically, I find myself bemused by the doctor's words, for I had already traversed the very experiences he listed. It is as if my latest concussion has acted as a catalyst, summoning forth the memories that the first had banished from my conscious mind. The cyclic nature of my condition, with its relentless back-and-forth, now presents itself as a peculiar twist of fate.

"As a result," he explains, "it is not uncommon to experience temporary gaps in your memory, particularly concerning recent events and personal experiences. These missing pieces may gradually return as your brain heals, but it is essential to remain vigilant and adhere to a proper recovery protocol."

The doctor's face softens, his gaze filled with empathy. "Rest assured, Mr. Hartwell, we will provide you with the best possible care and support throughout your recovery process."

"Thank you, doctor," I express, offering a small smile.

As the doctor exits the dull room, a surge of urgency wells up within me, compelling me to reach out to Sydney and bridge the chasm that has formed between us. The weight of lost memories burdens my mind, and an insatiable longing to reclaim what was once rightfully mine consumes me.

With a careful scan of the sterile hospital room, my eyes fall upon my belongings meticulously arranged on a nearby table. My outstretched fingers brush against the cool surface of my phone before grasping the device, feeling the familiar weight settle into my palm. Taking a deep breath, I dial Sydney's old number, the digits now etched indelibly into my memory.

In a hushed, desperate voice, I implore, "Please, Sydney, pick up." With each ring, my anticipation intensifies.

Just as my hope begins to wane, the call finally connects. However, the anticipated moment is abruptly shattered by an unexpected voice that interjects, intruding upon the solitude of my room.

My heart thumps aggressively as I shift my attention to the doorway. Before me, a figure emerges, revealing the unmistakable form of my mother. Her presence, though unexpected, brings a sense of momentary comfort, but then the anger over my last ten years of lost time begins to brew.

Time seems to momentarily stand still as my eyes take in her appearance. Her once-flowing chestnut hair has long since faded, now streaked with strands of silver. Lines of worry etch her face, bearing witness to the passage of years. Her eyes, once vibrant and full of life, now hold a hint of sadness and regret. What might my mother be regretting?

"Gabriel, how are you?" she asks. Her delicate hand reaches out, hesitating slightly before gently brushing against my cheek.

A myriad of emotions swirl within me as I absorb the sight of her. I find myself caught between the overwhelming desire to embrace her and the lingering bitterness of unanswered questions. I hesitate for a moment, struggling to find the right words. "I've been better," I finally reply curtly, "but, Mother, care to explain why you cut off my communication with Sydney for all these years?" I inquire, my voice quivering with hurt and indignation.

A flicker of surprise dances across her face, momentarily overshadowing the concern that had brought her to my bedside.

"So, you remember." She surveys me, then continues. "It's quite obvious she wasn't good for you, and I saw an opportunity to separate you both," she confesses, settling herself at the edge of my bed and leaning back.

"Not this again," I scoff, my laughter carrying a bitter tone as I shake my head in disbelief. "I don't care what you think about her, mother. I never did, and you have no right to impose your inability to accept her on me."

Engaging in any conversation with her feels like an exercise in futility. My mother is immovable in her beliefs, even when they are clearly misguided, and now those misguided beliefs have exacted a heavy toll on my life. She quite literally took advantage of my memory loss to obtain the outcome she desired.

Sensing the need to distance myself from her presence, I gently shift on the bed, moving my legs to the edge as I prepare to get up. The urge to find Sydney is growing stronger within me, overshadowing any desire to remain entangled in this futile debate.

"What's so attractive about Sydney Pearce? It will serve you to know I was always right about her. She's a cunning woman who stops at nothing for the sake of money," my mother spits bitterly, her harsh words steering my anger even stronger.

"That is enough," I bite back.

She pauses momentarily, her tone suddenly shifting to a calmer demeanor that only heightens the unsettling feeling that has seeped into the hospital room. It is as if she holds a secret, something significant she is about to reveal.

"Are you aware..." she begins, her words hanging in the air, laden with a weight I can't quite comprehend. But I have no desire to. However, courtesy demands I at least engage in the conversation.

"Of what?" I inquire, my hand instinctively running through my hair as I stand up, my other grabbing the bed rail to steady myself.

"Sydney married Brad, your best friend in college," she reveals. Time seems to freeze as her words sink in, casting a chilling stillness over my entire body. The room seems to shrink around us as if closing in on the impending revelation.

I can't believe what I'm hearing. It has to be some twisted attempt by my mother to manipulate me, to inflict further pain.

It seems inconceivable. Brad was my best friend, someone I had spent countless hours with, sharing laughter and secrets. Sydney, on the other hand, had always shown a clear distaste for his personality. The very idea is absurd.

"Stop making such horrid jokes, Mother," I retort playfully in an attempt to shake off the idea. I can't bear to entertain the possibility that her words hold any truth. With determination, I stride toward the rest of my belongings, eager to strip out of the hospital gown.

My mother's voice breaks through my inner turmoil, her words piercing through the air with haunting clarity. "It was a year after your accident. They had a son, Damon, and he will be turning ten soon. No one can get pregnant that fast, dear."

The room seems to spin around me as the full weight of her words crashes over me like a tsunami. Some things begin to align, and the denial shielding me from the truth shatters.

"Damon is my world."

"He's ten years old and has been the sole reason I've been holding on for quite some time now."

"I would like to talk about him with you, I would, but..."

"I... I can't share much about him. It's complicated."

The pieces fall into place, and the reasons behind Sydney's reservations and the awkwardness in her demeanor begin to make sense. It was guilt that had weighed heavily on her heart.

The cold reality settles on my shoulders, a heaviness I can't escape. Sydney and Brad, the two people I trusted the most, had found solace in each other's arms while I had been trapped in a haze of forgotten memories.

Images flash before my mind's eye, memories tainted by newfound knowledge. Sydney's smiles, once so genuine and full of warmth, now seem laden with hidden meanings. Brad's camaraderie, once a source of unwavering support, now feels like a facade masking his true intentions. How long had this betrayal been festering in the shadows, unbeknownst to me?

I stand there, paralyzed by the revelation, a storm of emotions swirling within me. The pain of betrayal, the loss of what once was, and the overwhelming feeling of being left behind merged into a maelstrom of anguish.

"Gabriel?" My mother's voice rings out, momentarily piercing the air before fading into the background as I fight to regain control of my breathing. The urgency in her tone carries a primal weight, a call that demands my attention.

I find myself unable to acknowledge her presence at the moment. Isn't this what she has wanted all along?

As the world around me blurs, my chest constricts, and I instinctively clutch at it, locking my teeth together tightly, determined to hold back the torrent of emotions threatening to spill forth. No, I will not allow myself to break down, not until I have confronted both of them, not until they have offered their explanations, and not until they have admitted their betrayal to my face!

CHAPTER 16

Sydney

I step into PTX's building, allowing the front door to swing shut behind me. Instantly, my attention is captured by the pacing silhouette of Jane.

Her demeanor appears peculiar, causing a slight furrowing of my brows. It seems rather early in the day for there to be a catastrophe. I hope that whatever situation has arisen is not a matter of life or death and does not directly involve me.

"Miss Pearce!" Jane's whispering voice reaches my ears, carrying an undertone of urgency. The echoing clicking of her footsteps on the tiled floor follows as she hurries toward me. Undeterred, I continue toward my office, my black bag swinging rhythmically by my left side while she trails behind.

"I should request the short version, but I suspect that may only serve to further confuse me," I prompt, eager for her to reveal the nature of the issue. "So, what seems to be the problem?"

"Well, first off, you should know that shortly after your departure yesterday, a man collapsed right in front of the building. We called 911, and they rushed him to the hospital," Jane explains in hurried breaths, her words almost tumbling over one another.

Halting my stride, I turn to face her directly. "What was wrong with him? Was he a patient?" The question escapes my lips, curiosity overshadowing the urgency of the situation. I take a breath and refocus on the matter that I still don't understand. "More importantly," I say, resuming my path to my office, "how does that relate to the situation at hand that clearly has you so worked up?"

"Well, yes... he's a patient but... right now he's in your office, Miss Pearce," Jane divulges in a sharp tone, causing me to abruptly halt again.

"What? What does he want from me? Is he planning on suing us for his incident or something of that nature?" Without granting Jane an opportunity to respond, I hasten my steps toward my office, a sense of urgency propelling me forward. Being sued would be bad PR for the company. I can't let that happen.

Yet, my hastened steps only seem to agitate Jane further. "Miss Pearce, please wait! There's more!" she calls out, struggling to match my pace. "He's in there with Mr. Romero, and they seem to be having some sort of a confrontation!" Her words echo in my ears, coinciding with the distinct sound of familiar voices.

I can't imagine what in the world my ex, Brad, is doing at my office. He certainly did not inform me he was coming in today.

"I met her first! You had no right to approach her!" Brad's tone resonates with aggravated fervor, catching me off guard. However, it isn't the sudden outburst that surprises me the most.

"What are you insinuating, Brad?" The composed yet weary-sounding undertone of the other man starkly contrasts Brad's aggression, and I am overwhelmed by the familiarity.

Gabriel. Gabe is right there!

126

But in the same breath at the sudden awareness of his presence, my legs turn to stone, rooted in place before the door. My fingers halt their reach for the handle as yet another surprise hits me.

He is addressing Brad!

"Gabe, before I even had the chance to make a move on her, you suddenly entered the picture," Brad goes on to explain. "Years without a chance, so can you blame me for seizing the opportunity that presented itself?" He lets out a bitter laugh.

What is he going on about precisely? Met me first? Take what chance? What exactly are they talking about?

"I have you to thank Gabe and, of course, your mother. She made it remarkably effortless to keep the two of you apart in the long run. I had a beautiful marriage, by the way," Brad continues, and at that very moment, I realize I need to speak up.

Brad's revelations and his choice of words insinuate that he might have played a role in my strained distance from Gabe all along. He had been there, disguising himself as a friend, the sole person I believed I could rely on. Meanwhile, he was part of the reason for my despair.

I married Brad because of the moments we shared and the support he gave me following Gabe's accident. Then, we raised Damon together! Were all those experiences built on a foundation of lies? Had I been unknowingly entangled in his web of deceit, eating his lies like a starved child?

I push open the heavy glass doors of my office, immediately commanding the attention of the two men within. Their faces betray their animosity, casting an oppressive atmosphere over the room. They stand face-to-face, their positions reflecting the simmering tension between them.

A pang of concern surges within me upon catching sight of Gabe. Pale and haggard, he does not look well.

An instinct urges me to rush to his side, yet the steely glare in his eyes conveys a clear message of deterrence, compelling me to maintain my distance.

"Gabe," I begin, intending to address him, but my words are abruptly cut off by Brad's interjection.

"Sydney!" Brad's voice slices through the air, carrying a noticeable tone of surprise. It seems absurd that he didn't expect me to enter my own office.

Brad steps forward, closing the gap between us with an unsteady gait. A subtle movement of his Adam's apple betrays his nerves as he swallows, and then he speaks, his words stumbling out. "Gabe... He remembers..." he trails off.

Reactively, I shift away, instinctively avoiding any physical contact. I intend to return to whatever Brad said before I entered, but now was not the time. My focus remains fixed on Gabe. "I know. I heard," I reveal.

"Sydney," Brad pleads, his voice cracking. "Please let me explain. There are details you need to know."

For a fleeting moment, my attention wavers, torn between the weight of Brad's words and the overpowering presence of Gabe. With each passing second, the gravity of the situation grows more pronounced, demanding an immediate resolution.

Though fatigue clouds Gabe's gaze, it still holds an intensity that pierces my heart. His lips part, but no words emerge. His sudden silence is taunting. What does he have to say to me now that he remembers us?

"Gabe," I approach him, my voice maintaining a steady tone, though tinged with the underlying anxiety pulsating within me.

"Why? Of all the people in the world, why chose each other? Of all the hearts in the world to break, you chose mine?" His words escape his lips, heavy with confusion and the unmistakable sting of betrayal that immediately echoes through my mind.

Silence lingers, thickening the atmosphere as Gabe momentarily averts his gaze, his brows knitting together. It appears as though conflicting desires battle within him, torn between demanding answers and grappling with the overwhelming surge of emotions that must be churning within him.

As I observe him, a pang of empathy tugs at my heart. I can't fathom the depths of his anguish nor the burdens he currently bears from the sudden revelations of all his memories. I sense his profound sense of isolation, and every fiber of my being yearns to offer solace, to wrap him in a comforting embrace.

But before I can respond, Brad scoffs, a derisive sound interjecting through the tense atmosphere. I glance at Brad as he turns toward Gabe, his eyes narrowing with defiance. "And why do you think you have the right to question us?" Brad's voice drips with sarcasm, his tone challenging and unyielding.

Has Brad always been this insufferable?

My patience wanes, my anger simmering beneath the surface. I step back toward Brad, facing his tall frame, my voice laced with a firmness that leaves no room for argument. "Brad, leave. Now," I command. It is my office, after all.

Brad's reaction is swift. His face twists in anger and disbelief, his hands curling into fists at his sides. For a moment, he stands there, his body tense with pent-up frustration. Then, with a dismissive shake of his head, he turns on his heel and strides out the door with a huff.

The room falls into an uneasy silence as the heavy glass doors swing shut behind Brad, leaving Gabe and me alone. My attention returns to Gabe, his presence still casting a shadow over the room. His weary eyes bore into mine, his face etched with exhaustion.

"Gabe, a lot happened in the aftermath of your accident." I struggle to find the right words as I attempt to explain. "Coming to terms with the harsh reality was hard, but with Brad around, it was somewhat bearable. The world continued its relentless march forward. But me? I was stuck. The days blurred into one another. I had nothing and no one. I had to start over. It was draining and crushingly hard."

I am slowly starting to find my words, and I pick up on Gabe's attentive demeanor, indicating his willingness to listen. However, I fail to recognize that he may not fully understand the message I'm trying to convey.

"So, the next best course of action was to move on with my best friend? To marry him and live your lives while I remained trapped in ignorance for ten whole years?" Gabe's cold words reach me as he chuckles, his laughter carrying a bitter tone. "Isn't that a little too convenient?"

His accusations cut me deeply, his words inflicting pain. It seems easier for him to stand there and let those words escape his mouth because he simply doesn't know. How could he? He wasn't there; that was the problem in the first place. Isn't that how we ended up here, screaming at each other?

"You have no idea," I begin, my voice breaking as bitter feelings churn within me, violently roiling my insides. "You have no idea what it was like searching for you, attempting to reach you with the limited resources I had."

The emotions I experienced back then, the challenging situations I endured, the things I lost, and the people who abandoned me after I had lost my mind trying to contact Gabe—all of it rushing back to me at once, crashing against me violently.

"When I found out I was pregnant, I lost my track scholarship. My family, you know how conservative they are... they turned their back on me, and I lost sight of myself for months because I dropped everything, absolutely everything, while desperately looking for you."

I pause to rein in my anger. He continues to glare at me.

"It took my entire life falling apart before I even began to accept the reality of you forgetting me, forgetting us. I would wait in our apartment, yearning for you to walk through those doors, but you never did!" I jab my finger into his chest, peering deeply into his glazed eyes.

Gabe's laughter erupts, his chest shaking as the sound reverberates through the room, leaving me unsettled and cold. What could he find funny about any of this?

"So, I'm supposed to believe that you were waiting for me?" he manages to utter between fits of laughter. "Enough with the bullshit, Sydney *Romero*!" he retorts sharply, emphasizing my last name. I resist the urge to flinch, clenching my jaw.

"You moved on rather quickly, and you even had a child together. Or am I expected to disregard the existence of your ten-year-old son?" His words carry a frigid edge.

I fall silent, unable to muster the strength to explain any further. It is apparent. Gabe has made up his mind about what he believes occurred. Trying to explain all the intricacies of our relationship seems pointless when he has his mind locked onto this crazy idea.

"You are nothing but a traitor, Sydney Romero," he spits, his voice dripping with disdain. His words resonate within the confines of my office, echoing off the walls and sinking deep into my wounded heart. "A traitor who never loved me."

A surge of pain washes over me, threatening to drown my resolve. How could he reduce our shared history, the love we once had, to such a damning accusation? My breath catches in my throat as I struggle to hold back tears that threaten to betray my composure.

Before I can muster any response, Gabe turns on his heel, his green eyes uncharacteristically devoid of any warmth, and begins to walk away. The ache in my chest intensifies as I watch him retreat, the distance between us widening with each step.

"Save your explanations," he spits, his voice laced with bitterness. "They will do you no good. My mother was right all along." His words hang in the air like a final verdict, a proclamation of his judgment, as he storms out of the room.

Tears well up in my eyes, blurring my vision as I stand there, immobile, devastated, and completely heartbroken. I clutch my trembling hands to my chest, a feeble attempt to contain the overwhelming emotions coursing through me.

The reality of losing Gabe once again, this time with the added knowledge of his belief in my betrayal, is a bitter pill to swallow, yet a wave of anger overshadows it all.

Gabe really believes I betrayed him?

A sudden crash followed by shouting interrupts my spiral. "No! Mr. Hartwell!" Jane exclaims. "Call 911!"

CHAPTER 17

Sydney

"You are nothing but a traitor, Sydney Romero. A traitor who never loved me."

"Save your explanations. They will do you no good. My mother was right all along."

His words were so cruel, too cruel. Calling me Sydney *Romero* stings. After enduring everything I went through following his accident. I do not deserve such cruelty.

Understanding Gabe's experiences and challenges is far beyond my reach. I know I cannot fully grasp the magnitude of what he endured. The process of regaining memories lost a decade ago, only to discover that his closest friend had married his intended spouse, was an emotional maelstrom I can never expect to fully comprehend.

However, amid the swirling tumult of emotions, it feels as though Gabe had been hasty in leaping to conclusions about my relationship with Brad without even listening to anything I had to say. My story should be the one he wants to hear, but he seems to believe whatever lies Brad told him before I arrived.

Yes, I did marry Brad. Yes, we raised Damon together, but there is so much more to the story. There are so many other factors that still have the potential to turn all our lives upside down, and I am not prepared to face any of them at the moment.

After witnessing Brad's newfound cynicism, I suspect he may have distorted the truth, misleading Gabe into believing our marriage was built on love. Yet, considering the depth of Gabe's knowledge of me, he should have discerned from the outset that such assumptions were far from accurate.

In truth, my heart belongs solely to Gabe, and he occupies an irreplaceable spot within it. Our bond is unwavering, a cherished connection I thought we both understood. Despite the circumstances that led to my marriage to Brad, I made deliberate efforts to convey my feelings to him, ensuring Brad understood my enduring affection for Gabe.

It was astonishing how readily Gabe labeled me a traitor, as if everything else pales in comparison. It seems he believes I had moved on too quickly. The audacity of his accusations leaves me reeling, struggling to comprehend his perspective.

"You are nothing but a traitor, Sydney Romero." His words echo in my thoughts, a painful reminder of the depth of his condemnation. It fuels an anger that smolders beneath the surface. I scoff, a brief exhalation of disbelief escaping my lips. I am unable to contain the frustration welling up within me, even as I stand, feet planted on the floor of my office.

Hours have passed since Gabe departed in an ambulance, after collapsing *in* office, this second time. We learned he checked himself out of the hospital prematurely. Nevertheless, he has left me alone in a whirlwind of conflicting emotions. As I find myself in this all-too-familiar predicament of losing Gabe yet again, my eyes sweep across the room, momentarily fixating on the arranged items adorning my desk.

Unconsciously, my fists clench as a surge of heat courses through my fingertips. The weight of betrayal, both real and perceived, bears heavily upon my shoulders, fueling the fire of my anger.

Among the carefully arranged items, a document lays conspicuously on my office table–Larissa Hartwell's proposal for PTX's sponsorship. It presents a potential opportunity, albeit at an inconvenient time.

Gabe's accusations will not deter me. If he is determined to believe I betrayed him, so be it. In a burst of frustration, I swiftly seize the document, crumpling its pristine surface in my clenched grip. The crunching sound of creasing paper echoes in the room, mirroring my tumultuous emotions.

My anger propels me forward, driving me to a hasty decision. I make my way to my desk, gripping the document securely in my hand. Without hesitation, I swiftly pull a pen from the drawer, ready to inscribe my name onto the paper. As I forcefully press the pen against the document, my signature emerges in bold and deliberate strokes. Each letter seems to embody the intensity of my anger, the ink serving as a testament to my frustration and unwavering determination.

My decisions should not solely be influenced by the circumstances surrounding my relationship with Gabe. Instead, they should serve as an assertion of my mastery over my own life. Placing the now-signed document back on my desk, I face it.

Have I made the right choice? I ponder quietly, doubting my decision. The question lingers timidly in my mind, begging for an answer.

The familiar sound of doors swinging open reaches me. Intrigued, I adjust my position on my feet to steal a glimpse of the unexpected visitor who dares to enter my office unannounced.

A chill creeps down my spine as a cold sensation rushes through me, temporarily numbing the sudden surge of anger at the sight of her.

Sara fucking Jensen.

I calmly articulate my request, careful not to let my recent frustration taint the conversation. "Please provide me with three reasons, Sara, why I should refrain from pursuing legal action regarding your blatant breach of our contractual agreement."

As I await her response, I maintain a composed demeanor, fully aware of the significance this discussion holds for both of us. With an air of unease, Sara shifts on her feet, her bright blue eyes darting momentarily to the floor before meeting my gaze again.

"First," she begins her statement with a soft, gentle voice, slightly wavering, "I am deeply sorry for any inconvenience my actions may have caused. I deeply regret the unintended consequences that have potentially compromised our professional relationship and violated the terms we previously established."

"Surely, you didn't anticipate a mere apology would have any influence on me, Sara. Your experience working alongside me should have made it clear that any apology would fall short," I assert confidently, intertwining my hands and leaning against the desk for support. "Explain yourself."

Sara's head hangs low, her long, curly chestnut tresses falling across her face.

"May I, Sydney?" she asks, gesturing toward the maroon sofa positioned against the pristine gray wall of my office.

Surprised by her request, I nod slightly and respond, "Certainly, you may sit."

As Sara approaches the couch, her steps are cautious, her movements tentative. With grace, she lowers herself onto the plush cushion, her posture reflecting vulnerability. The material molds around her form, providing a supportive embrace.

Observing Sara's presence, I realize a marked change in her appearance. Her fair complexion now appears healthy and radiant, contradicting her tired demeanor before her disappearance. The lines of exhaustion have softened, replaced by a subtle glow of vitality.

Driven by curiosity, I muster the courage to approach the subject cautiously. "You look well. I am certain your absence played a part in this transformation. Would you care to share where you've been and why you abandoned your job?"

Sara's eyes briefly flicker with an indiscernible emotion as she inhales deeply, causing her chest to expand ever so slightly. "It all happened so fast. A few days before the new client was due to visit, I found myself in an unexpected situation," Sara begins, her voice full of hesitation as she twiddles her thumbs. "I needed time to think." Her words are barely audible, but even from a distance, I catch every word.

Sara had missed work because she needed time to think? It seems highly implausible. However, I decide to let her continue, curious to see where her story will lead.

"I have been seeing one of our clients secretly for some time now," Sara reveals, her tone tinged with resignation.

Normally, I'd be furious, but given my own emotional entanglement with Gabe, who am I to bring up how risky that type of behavior is for our company's reputation?

"And," she continues, her tone shifting, "we found out I was pregnant. We'd been having some problems with the relationship before that, so finding out I was carrying his baby made me question everything. I wasn't sure what I wanted to do."

Our eyes meet, and Sara confesses, "I suppose I should have mentioned during all those times you asked if I was all right that I wasn't. I was scared to tell you because he is a big client for us."

Her confession stirs a slight tug in my heart. Perhaps I would have eased up the workload if I had known.

"I have decided to stay with him, and we will raise our child together. He's currently waiting outside the door to hear from you," Sara laughs nervously.

I straighten my posture, taken aback by her revelation. She must be joking.

The room is interrupted by a muffled knock, and the doors creak open. Jane enters, wearing a wide grin on her face.

"Miss Pearce, Mr. Maxwell has requested I tell you to take it easy on," she coughs softly, casting a knowing glance toward Sara, who sits up in anticipation, "and I quote, *his lady*."

As the request is relayed to me by Jane, my attention shifts from her to Sara, who sits across from me, cheeks tugged upward as a smile rests on her lips. It is a noticeable contrast to her nervous demeanor just moments ago.

I take a moment to observe Sara again, her fair complexion glowing with a subtle radiance. The transformation in her appearance intrigues me, prompting me to consider the reality of her story and her reasons for her sudden absence.

As I think about her reasoning, a twinge of empathy creeps into my heart. It becomes evident that Sara hadn't abandoned me as I had initially believed. Rather, circumstances beyond her control had led her on this unforeseen path.

I can't help but draw parallels between her experiences and my own tumultuous journey with Gabe. Like Sara, I have faced unexpected twists and turns, finding myself entangled in a web of emotions and choices that led me to where I stand today.

Maybe our stories aren't as different as they seem. I might even owe her a sense of gratitude. Surprisingly, her absence led me to an unexpected meeting, one that stirred the depths of my soul with a profound wave of emotions. Her absence led me back to Gabe.

However, it appears that I have lost him once more, with little chance of sharing any future moments together. I scribbled my signature on Larissa's proposal, seemingly cementing this harsh reality. What have I done?

Shaking myself out of the increasing chokehold of my regrets, I redirect my attention to Sara.

Meeting Sara's gaze, I speak in a hushed tone, my words imbued with a genuine understanding. "Sara, while I'm sorry you had to go through so much uncertainty, I do understand why you needed to withdraw. I am grateful for your honesty. We have both weathered unforeseen circumstances in our lives this past month."

Her brows furrow in response to my statement. Ignoring her inquisitive gaze, I continue, "While I may not yet grasp the full extent of it all, I now realize that your absence was not solely your own doing."

A sense of relief washes over her face, replacing the tension that had been present earlier.

"It appears that everything has worked out in the end. PTX has secured the sponsorship," I disclose, nodding.

As soon as the words leave my mouth, a bright grin illuminates her face. She jumps out of her seat, exclaiming, "Really? That's incredible! You're finally getting everything you've been striving for. I'm so happy for you, Sydney."

But have I truly achieved everything I desire? The truth is that it feels like I have suffered even greater losses. Over the past month, I have experienced the return of Gabe in my life and entertained a secret relationship with him. At one point, he had been the love of my life, and even now, I cannot deny the feelings that linger within me.

Yet now he has walked away, convinced I betrayed him with his closest friend. He has labeled me a traitor, accusing me of never truly loving him, and it has deeply wounded me. I resent that he could doubt my love for him so easily, questioning the authenticity of our past relationship without understanding the events that unfolded before my marriage to Brad.

Sure, amid my anger, I had convinced myself that I would be fine without him. Yet I know that is not true at all. I must find a way to explain my past decisions to him. I can't let Gabe believe this lie he has conjured without knowing the truth.

CHAPTER 18

Gabriel

"I trust you've learned your lesson about doing too much too soon. Please ensure that you take it easy at home, Mr. Hartwell," the doctor advises. His customary white coat rustles with each movement as he removes the IV drip from my hand. I've been here for four days. It is a bright, sunny Tuesday, and I am more than ready to get out of here.

Slowly and cautiously, I climb down from the hospital bed, my weakened limbs protesting with every step. The sterile linoleum floor feels cool against my bare feet as I approach one of the attending nurses.

"Excuse me," I address the nurse, my voice still weak from days of limited use, "where are my clothes?"

The nurse, a stern-faced woman with gentle brown eyes, nods. "Yes, Mr. Hartwell," she confirms with a warm smile. "Your clothes are in the closet in the bathroom. Take your time to change, and let us know if you need any assistance."

Grateful for her assurance, I enter the bathroom, the door creaking as it closes behind me. The harsh fluorescent light illuminates the small space, casting a glow over everything within. I catch a glimpse of my reflection in the mirror; my face looks weary and marred by the emotional battles it has endured.

As I change out of the scratchy hospital gown, my mind wanders to the events of the past four days. The constant monitoring of my brain activity by the doctors, the wires and sensors attached to my temples, and the beeping machines serve as guardians of my fragile existence. It all seems like a hazy dream, a surreal experience that now feels oddly distant.

But amid the fog of my thoughts, one figure stands out with unwavering clarity: Sydney. The woman I had loved and trusted, only to discover her deep betrayal. Despite the anger that lingers within me, I can't deny the longing that tugs at my heart whenever she crosses my mind.

I acknowledge the paradox of my emotions, the bitterness and the longing existing side by side. Sydney has hurt me deeply, yet she occupies a space in my heart that seems reserved exclusively for her. Even in my most tired state, I can't escape the truth—I miss her dearly and desperately.

With a sigh, I finish changing into my clothes, embracing the familiarity and comfort they provide. The hospital attire, though necessary for my recovery, has served as a constant reminder of my vulnerability and dependence.

As I step out of the bathroom, I feel a renewed sense of autonomy, a small victory in the face of adversity. I have, after all, fully regained all my memories, even the ones I would have loved to lose to ignorance.

My attention is immediately drawn to my mother's presence. It has become a frequent habit of hers to visit me, though she claims it is out of care. However, I have caught on to her true motives—she often asks about my other visitors.

"Gabriel, are you ready to go?" she asks, breaking the silence. "Katie has been quite moody lately. I'm sure she will be thrilled to see you." Her words continue to flow, accompanied by her unwavering formal composure that exudes a subtle mix of pride and arrogance.

Responding with a simple grunt, I lack the motivation to engage in conversation with her. We both step out of my assigned room, greeted by the sight of people hurriedly going about their activities. Among the commotion, a few stand out, contrasting the swift pace with their stillness.

Emerging from a corner, two nurses and a doctor catch my attention. They are carefully maneuvering a stretcher on which lays a young boy with a mop of dark hair. The rhythmic sound of their footfalls echoes through the corridor, creating an atmosphere of urgency.

Witnessing this scene evokes a deep sense of empathy as I watch their purposeful strides toward operating rooms further down the hall.

I observe as the medical professionals deftly navigate through the space. The boy, his features bearing traces of discomfort, lays motionless on the stretcher with blood coating his head. The gravity of the situation is palpable, and my heart aches for the young child and the challenges he is undoubtedly facing.

"I will be right back," my mother interjects, shifting my attention away from the boy.

"All right then," I reply, watching as she strolls down the hall, pressing her phone against her ear.

Heading in the opposite direction, I round the same corner from which the boy had been hauled. Suddenly, I collide with something—or, rather, someone.

My pulse quickens as I turn to face the woman before me. Tears streaming down her cheeks, her familiar hazel eyes gaze into mine, widening in surprise.

"Sydney?"

CHAPTER 19

Sydney

I'm enjoying a pleasant day off and relishing the opportunity to have some time to myself. Tuesdays are slow for us at PTX, so I don't feel guilty taking a little time to myself.

On Monday, I received a response from Larissa regarding the approval of the sponsorship and the commencement of the process. With that news in mind, I decided to take a break from work the next day before diving into our getting the expansion planned and completed. I need my wits about me for this expansion.

Once I drop Damon off at school, I dedicate the day to journaling to clarify my thoughts and then tackling various household chores. I have also found over the years that writing in my journals settles me. I haven't journaled since the day before the helicopter ride to Gabe's estate.

Now, here I am, clad in a comfy sweats, sipping my third cup of coffee as I lounge by my kitchen table, ready to write my thoughts for today. A wave of nostalgia washes over me, prompting my mind to meander down the corridors of memory, eventually settling on thoughts of Gabe. It only days since he collapsed at PTX, and the image of him that lingers in my recollections stirs a genuine concern within me.

The memory of his worn-out expression and the slight hunch of his shoulders flashes before my eyes. Even though he called me a traitor, should I risk reaching out to him? Uncertainty dances in my mind as I weigh the pros and cons of contacting him.

"Why? Of all the people in the world, you chose each other? Of all the hearts in the world to break, you chose mine?"

"So, the next best course of action was to move on with my best friend? To marry him and live your lives while I remained trapped in ignorance for ten whole years?"

Gabe's words keep chanting in my head. I must find a way to contact him. We need a chance to talk. I need to tell him the truth.

I reach for my phone, my fingertips gliding over the sleek, cool casing. Just as I pick it up, it rings, interrupting my thoughts. Surprise washes over me, as I read the name on the screen.

Mrs. Sanders. Damon's homeroom teacher.

Inhaling deeply, I glide my finger across the screen and bring the phone up to my ear, bracing myself for whatever news awaits me on the other end of the call. I hope that Damon, my normally well-behaved son, has not found himself in any sort of trouble.

"Mrs. Romero," Mrs. Sanders began, her shaky voice resonating through the speakers of my phone.

I'm about to correct her, but the next set of words that echo through the phone halt any intention to speak.

"Damon... well, Damon has just been urgently taken to Sharp Memorial hospital."

With trembling hands, put her on speaker and hastily fumble through a drawer in search of my keys, my heart thudding against my ribcage like a primal drum.

"He had an accident. It appears he lost his balance and tumbled down an entire flight of stairs, severely injuring his head. I'm so sorry, Mrs. Romero."

Time seems to stretch infinitely as I pull on clothes and urgently dart out of the house, my mind awash with a torrent of worries that race through my thoughts. Outside, the world seems to blur. Fear mingles with determination, propelling me forward.

I climb into my car and begin speeding toward the hospital, my mind racing through a whirlwind of possibilities. What could have happened to Damon? How did he fall down the stairs? Questions without answers haunt my every thought, intensifying the unease that grips my heart.

As I approach the hospital, my heart pounds in my chest, matching the urgency of my thoughts. The world outside blurs into a mosaic of fleeting colors as my car races through the city streets. My knuckles turn white as I clench my fists, attempting to maintain composure amid the mounting unease. I slide the car awkwardly into a parking spot and run for the Emergency doors.

Every second counts, and my focus is solely on reaching Damon. With trembling hands, I impatiently push forward the glass revolving door, the cool air of the hospital embracing me with its clinical scent. It's the Emergency but there seems to be an extremely high number of waiting patients, many on stretchers. I hurry toward the intake desk. But before I can reach it, my heart seizes in my chest, freezing me in place. There, being wheeled in into the corridor on a stretcher, is Damon, his small figure obscured by a flurry of medical personnel.

"Damon!" I cry out, my tone colored with pure desperation to hold my son.

The doctors and nurses surrounding Damon pause momentarily, their eyes turning toward me. Their expressions momentarily convey their curiosity. One doctor, her face etched with concern, approaches me.

"I'm Dr. Roberts. You are...?" she asks, her voice steady yet compassionate amid the chaos.

My voice trembles as I reply, "I'm Damon Romero's mother. What will happen to my son? Is he going to be alright?"

The doctor's gaze holds mine briefly, her eyes reflecting a wealth of knowledge and responsibility. She quickly assesses the gravity of the situation.

"From what we know, he experienced a fall down an entire flight of stairs, the force of which directly impacted his head, resulting in a serious injury we're monitoring carefully. We are working to ensure his well-being. There is the possibility of surgery—" I gasp, interrupting her. "Yes, Mrs. Romero, there is the possibility of surgery, and I must advise you we are in an unusual situation. We have to prioritize care and Damon is a high priority."

The doctor and nurses resume walking quickly with Damon's stretcher.

"Thank you. Wha—"

Dr. Roberts continues. "You may have sensed the heightened pitch in the ER. We're dealing with a multi-vehicle pileup on the Cabrillo Freeway. Even with helicopters, there might be some delay in getting enough blood to us. Would you and your family be willing to help out with a blood donation?"

"Yes, I'll donate. I'm Type A. Damon has a unique blood type, AB-negative; is that going to be a problem?"

"Not if we have enough Type O blood. That's a universal donor type. All blood types will help. And I suppose with Damon's rare type, if a family member AB-neg donates, we can use the Type O on hand for others. Anyone who's Type O will be in demand."

My mind races, trying to absorb Dr. Roberts' words. The urgency in her voice echoes in my ears. Without hesitation, I nod, determination fueling my response. "Yes, of course. Whatever it takes, I will find blood donors. Please, do everything you can to save him."

"Emergency will direct you. We must leave you here now."

As the doctors swiftly rush Damon towards the operating room area, I pause and wipe the moisture from my cheeks.

A nurse approaches me with a small yet comforting smile. "I hear Damon's blood is AB-negative. You said you are Type A. Damon's father must be Type AB-negative. Is he close by to help?" she asks.

"His father…," I began, my voice trembling, "his father is…"

I know Brad is also Type A, like me. The one person who has Damon's blood type is currently impossible to contact.

But Dr. Roberts did say any and all blood will help. Driven by a sense of urgency, I propel myself forward, determined to catch up with the doctor to get a better handle of Damon's prognosis before I call family and friends. I swiftly around a corner where Damon's gurney has just vanished from sight when, abruptly, a collision jolts me to a halt.

An upsurge of frustration surges within me, threatening to spill forth as harsh words against the person who had carelessly bumped into me. But as I turn to confront the culprit, my anger dissolves into astonishment.

Gabe. It's Gabe.

CHAPTER 20

Gabriel

Startled and surprised, I start to ask what's happening, but before I can say a word, Sydney grabs my wrist. Holding on tightly, she drags me along, her hurried pace testing my ability to keep up. It quickly becomes evident that we are heading toward the hospital's emergency intake area.

She releases her grip on my wrist as she arrives at the charge nurse's desk. Her frenzied movements and demeanor suggest distress. Questions overwhelm my thoughts. What happened? Why is she here, in the hospital?

The charge nurse glances up from her paperwork, her inquiring expression aimed at Sydney.

"I am Damon Romero's mother. I found a blood donor with his blood type," she exclaims, her voice trembling with urgency.

Blood donor? For Damon Romero?

"Damon is my world." The weight of Sydney's words reverberates within the recesses of my mind, instigating a profound realization. Damon Romero... Her son? Their son?

"Sydney, what exactly is happening?" I struggle to conceal my frustration.

"Gabe, I beg you, with everything I am, with everything we've shared, there isn't time to provide details. Please just do as I say right now," she pleads, desperation in her eyes. "My son's life depends on you."

"Wh-why does his life depend on me?"

"Gabe, please," she implores, her voice trembling with emotion. Hastily, she turns, facing me directly. Sydney extends her arm and places her palm on my chest. She takes a deep breath.

"I understand. This is difficult to comprehend, and I'm sorry for the lack of clarity," she murmurs, "Brad, he... he can't help. Damon had an accident, and he needs blood for surgery. The hospital is short of blood. I'm going to donate to help out, but I'm not type O, so I can't help Damon. You're a directly compatible donor, Gabe. I'm begging you, please save my son's life."

She pauses, and takes another deep breath."

"Please save your son's life."

"Over my dead body," my mother abruptly interrupts the conversation, her voice cutting through the air as her shoes click on the cool, tiled floor.

Sydney and I both turn to face her.

"Now's not the time to test me," Sydney says, her voice steady and firm, the underlying determination a surprise shift from just moments ago.

Even my mother, usually composed and confident, is taken aback by Sydney's response.

"You have quite the nerve!" my mother icily retorts, her voice dripping with hostility. Her eyes narrow, and she spits out her words, transmitting her disdain. "But then again, I am not surprised. You've always been nothing more than a bold leech, attaching yourself to Gabriel for your selfish gain."

Sydney's defiant gaze locks with Larissa's, her hazel eyes ablaze with visible anger. "I'm selfish? Have *you* ever taken a moment to think about the irreversible consequences of your actions?"

"Sydney!" Despite her unreasonable behavior, she is still my mother.

"What?" Sydney snaps back, her gaze full of fire, now directed at me.

My mother's face contorts with anger, her narrowed eyes glaring sharply back at Sydney. "How dare you speak to me in such a manner? You betrayed my son, and now you dare to lecture me?"

"Betrayed your son? The entire reason I married Brad in the first place was due to the desperate situation you, Larissa Hartwell, put me through. You blocked all my calls, ignored my messages, and disregarded my desperate pleas to speak with Gabe," Sydney continues, throwing accusations at my mother.

Although my mother clenches her jaw and squares her shoulders, exuding an air of contempt, she is not denying the accusations. The truth is undeniable–she had blocked Sydney's every attempt to reach me.

This revelation shakes me to my core. I realize that my mother had purposefully omitted this information when she previously disclosed Sydney's past marital status.

"Mother, you're the manipulative one. You've selectively revealed only the parts of Sydney's past that suit your agenda. What other secrets have you been keeping from me?"

CHAPTER 21

Sydney

Larissa ignores Gabe's accusations. "Well, I don't believe it. That can't be true. You're lying," Larissa retorts icily, trying to redirect the conversation.

Doubt is an integral part of Larissa Hartwell's nature. However, I know my words are the truth. Damon is, without a doubt, Gabe's son.

"Let's order DNA tests," I counter. "But after we donate our blood." I resist the urge to plead with her. It'll be wasted. She lacks empathy.

Larissa's voice, tinged with menace, issues a veiled warning, "If you are indeed lying, rest assured that I will not hesitate to ruin you." However, despite the undercurrent of authority in her tone, I perceive a subtle vulnerability, hinting that she is not entirely immune to the persuasive power of the notion she has a grandson.

With resolve in my heart, I turn to face Gabe, his green eyes blazing with anger at his mother.

Ignoring the curious onlookers and the whispers that dance in the air, I approach Gabe with steady steps and gently take his clenched hand in mine.

"Gabe, I know this is overwhelming. I will explain everything, but right now, Damon needs you. He needs your blood for a better chance of recovery. And if that's not enough, it'll help others too."

Gabe's troubled eyes search mine. He hesitates, his mind clearly churning. But as I gently squeeze his hand, an unspoken understanding passes between us.

"I will explain everything," I repeat in a whisper. "Gabe, let's go donate blood for our son."

With a deep breath, Gabe nods as if deciding to focus on what is most important first. The weight of the truth we carry looms over us all.

Gabe turns back to the nurse's desk; his steps are deliberate yet burdened. I follow closely behind, determined to see this through.

At the desk, the nurse greets us with an empathetic smile. Her eyes flicker with curiosity, sensing the gravity of the situation. I take a deep breath, gather my composure, and speak in a calm, assertive tone.

"We are here to donate blood, him directly for Damon Romero," I state. "I would also like to request a DNA test between the donor and the receiver."

The nurse nods. "The DNA test isn't an emergency test, but I'll get you a request form."

As I begin filling out the paperwork, I feel Larissa's icy glares directed toward me. I meet her gaze with unwavering resolve, my voice steady as I address her.

"Larissa, I understand your skepticism," I say, maintaining a composed demeanor, "but I assure you, a DNA test will confirm Damon's parentage."

Larissa's glare intensifies, her skepticism evident in her narrowed eyes. Yet, despite her disbelief, a hint of uncertainty lingers beneath the surface. The reality of the situation and the possibility that she might have a grandson from Gabe, a surprise male heir, really seems to be chipping away at her stubborn demeanor.

I return to the paperwork, carefully filling out the necessary details while my mind races with thoughts of my past. Stealing a glance at Gabe, who stands beside me, after each line I complete. His expression is a mosaic of emotions–shock, confusion, and a glimmer of something unfamiliar.

Once the forms are completed, I hand them back to the nurse, who reviews them with a practiced eye. Her gaze shifts briefly to Larissa, who continues to scrutinize our every move. Sensing the tension, the nurse maintains her professionalism, keeping any judgment or bias hidden behind a mask of neutrality.

"Very well," she states, clutching the documents tightly as she rises from her seat. With a composed demeanor, she motions for us to accompany her. "Follow me, Mr. Hartwell, Mrs. Romero."

With the nurse leading the way, Gabe and I follow her down a maze of sterile corridors. The fluorescent lights buzz overhead, casting a stark illumination on the path ahead. The air holds a distinctive scent–a blend of antiseptic and nervous anticipation. I exhale audibly, hoping to breathe out the nerves.

As we walk, the silence between us is thick with unspoken words. The weight of Damon's precarious condition hangs in the atmosphere, pushing us forward with a sense of urgency. I keep my gaze fixed on the nurse's back, determined to navigate this unfamiliar territory and secure the blood donation that will hopefully save our son's life.

Finally, we arrive at a nondescript door marked "Blood Donation." The nurse opens it with a gentle push, revealing a well-organized space bustling with medical professionals in white coats. The rhythmic sound of beeping machines and hushed conversations fill the room.

Another nurse approaches us, her demeanor calm and reassuring. She directs each of us towards a reclining chair, while another nurse prepares the necessary equipment for the blood donation.

I'm set up quickly, but Gabe's recent hospitalization must have triggered a precaution. The nurse thoroughly checks Gabe's vital signs to make sure he has recovered enough to donate. While she reviews his vitals and records, my donation is finished.

Satisfied, the nurse readies Gabe's donation equipment, her hands moving with precision and care. She positions the needle carefully, her touch gentle despite the task at hand. Gabe clenches his other hand, steeling himself for the slight discomfort that accompanies the process.

I hold my breath as the blood flows through the clear tubes, a tangible symbol of the connection between Gabe and Damon. Every drop represents a lifeline, bridging the gap between father and son. My heart swells with gratitude for this chance at a renewed bond, but the uncertainty of the situation still gnaws at the edges of my hopefulness.

Upon discovering the extent of my actions ten years ago, I wonder how he will react and if he will understand the reasons behind my actions. How much should I disclose? Will he empathize with the challenges I had faced, or will he focus only on my faults?

No, Gabe isn't like that. At least, he wasn't in the past. However, as the years have passed, the impact of his memory loss has definitely left its mark. Even though he has regained his memories, he is not merely the person who existed before the accident; the version of him that existed during that period of amnesia still lingers. His decisions now and in the future will be made from the entirety of his experiences.

I release a small exhale from my mouth. The situation isn't as straightforward as I had hoped. It's clear that I need to have a candid conversation with him, addressing the issue directly and truthfully.

Minutes pass like hours, and time seems to stretch as we wait for the donation to be completed. The machines' rhythmic beep and the medical staff's hushed voices create a symphony of tension that envelopes us. In this silent dance with fate, we can only pray that Damon's body will accept his father's gift.

Finally, the nurse removes the needle, her smile colored with compassion. Gabe lets out a deep sigh, relief in his eyes.

"All right then, that's it. We're all done," she says, breaking the settled silence.

"Thank you!" I breathe out, nervously adjusting the sleeves of my sweater, feeling the intensity of Gabe's gaze fixed upon me.

As soon as the nurse leaves, Gabe abruptly stands up, firmly taking hold of my wrist, and proceeds to pull me along with him. He tugs urgently, leading us to a room nearby.

Upon entering, I see the room is empty, a counseling room, a conversation room with a sofa and a couple of chairs. He quietly closes the door behind him, allowing the latch to click into place.

The atmosphere is thick with tension, creating a momentary stillness that seems to amplify the sound of our breathing, which is the only audible presence in the room.

"Why?" he begins, his voice carrying an unnerving, chilly undertone.

I swallow hard, mustering the courage to ask, "Why what?"

"Why did you hide the fact that I had a son?" he questions, his frustration evident.

CHAPTER 22

Gabriel

I should look away from them–her eyes.

The turbulent whirlpool of emotions within them is undeniably captivating, emanating a raw honesty that pulls me in deeper. It is as if that hazel gaze holds the power to shatter my emotional barriers, a prospect that leaves me uneasy.

The glistening moisture in her eyes tugs at my heartstrings. I can't stand the sight of tears. I can't bring myself to look away from her despite how painful it is to see her tears. Maintaining eye contact can lead to a vulnerability I'm not prepared to confront. I'm hurt and confused; a profound sense of being lost overwhelms me. An urgent yearning for an explanation gnaws at me as an inner violence seems to claw at my chest, seeking appeasement.

"You say it like I did it on purpose." Her response comes in a hushed mumble, and she averts her gaze from mine.

The weight of her statement lingers in the air, creating a subtle tension between us. I endeavor to speak, yet the words seem to entangle themselves in my throat. So, I inhale deeply to steady myself before finally finding my voice. "You know that is not what I mean."

"Are you sure? Your skepticism is painted all over your face." Her response is swift and sharp as she retorts.

I confess, "I am frustrated, Sydney. It has been ten long years without you. We had dreams and plans. We were going to get married.

"I know, Gabe, and that is the most painful part. I have always known." Her voice chokes with emotion as she meets my gaze once again. "You were unreachable after the accident. Do you have any idea what it felt like for me back then? Not knowing if you were recovering. I heard Blake and Ella died in the accident. You had suddenly disappeared from the face of the earth, leaving me utterly shattered. And then finding out I was pregnant. Having to sort all that out by myself."

Tears cascade down her cheeks as she speaks, and her voice trembles. "I had been so excited to tell you. I needed you. But I couldn't find you, didn't know if you were... alive." Her voice ends in a whisper.

Reaching out, I cupped her cheeks with both hands, using my thumbs to brush away her tears. "Sydney," I say her name like I need to hear it, and when I pull her in, I kiss her like I need to know she's real.

She doesn't react at first; then, she's pushing into me all at once. I fall back, sitting on the closest armchair in this room, a counseling room used for private conversation, and like a man possessed, I need to have one of those with her right now.

"Sydney," I say her name again as our lips separate, our breaths mixing, and her hands slide under my shirt as mine race up her back. They curl at the top of her shoulders as she knells and straddles me in the chair, and I pull her down tight against me, against the hardened length in my pants.

There's no question if we should do this here. There's just the clumsy way our mouths come together again, the taste of her filling my head, how her fingers are now working my belt loose.

I slip a hand into her hair, liberating it from the hair tie. While fighting her tongue for dominance, I flick my thumb over the cup of her bra where her nipple is pebbled beneath. She moans into my mouth, and the vibration of it threatens to overrun the rest of my thoughts as I swallow the noise.

My belt clanks too loudly against the arm of the chair, and we break apart, startled by the noise, by the reckless way we're acting. But we didn't get a chance before, it was stripped away from us, and we both know it now.

With her gorgeous eyes on mine, she slips her hand into my pants, pushing my boxers down, her fingers curling around my length, and I swallow the way my heartbeat threatens to choke me as she pumps her slender fingers around me.

I'm already so hard it's almost painful, and like she knows, she makes sure to run her thumb along the underside of my cock, the sensitive head, making me twitch.

"Syd—"

"Shh. I'm hungry." She uses my words back to me as she cuts me off, and God help me–I have to clench my jaw to keep from groaning as she slides back onto her knees, lowering her head down and wrapping her warm, wet mouth around me.

I struggle not to buck up, my hand in her hair tightening slightly as she consumes me, her tongue working along me like she's savoring a decadent dessert. My eyes roll in my skull, my hips rising slowly with the tortuous motion of her mouth.

Her hand moves from the base of my cock so she can push past her own physical comfort, and her mouth tightens as she swallows around me before she pulls back with a faint *pop* as she looks up at me through her lashes.

I shiver down to my toes from that look, then my hands are on her hips, pulling her forward.

"I'm not done," she protests.

"Me either," I assure her as I throw up a thank you to the heavens that she wore loose shorts. I slip them to the side, her panties, and find her already wet for me, so ready.

I push her shorts, panties down to her thighs, and bouncing my knees, I bring her forward again, nestling the length of my cock between her netherlips, letting her watch over the ridge of her shorts on her thighs as I slide against them a few times before I tip it down enough to push inside of her.

Her arms wrap around my neck, and I move my hand to her mouth, covering it as I rest our foreheads together, giving her another solid bounce so gravity makes me hilt inside of her. This time, her moan is muffled against my fingers, and I curl my other arm around her waist tightly, taking control.

The plush curve of her butt bounces against my thighs as I raise her and press her back down, stifling my own groans the best I can. Her knees squeeze my hips when I move my hand, and she presses her chest to mine.

She rises then on her own, helping my grip on her as she sinks down on me, rises back up, sinks down again, and then rolls her hips, causing friction without ever letting me out of her confining walls.

"Gabe." Her gasp is soft against my ear out of necessity, but I can hear the desperation in her voice as I set both of my hands on her hips, holding her in place, and drive up into her with short, muffled claps of our flesh meeting.

Those lovely lips that I'd been missing without realizing it find my neck, pressing against it, causing goosebumps to rise down my arms, and I thrust harder, pushing her up to that peak that I want to tumble over the edge with her when she arrives.

Hearts pounding together in our chests, indiscernible from each other's, her lips press back to mine as her inner walls flex, and I pull her down flush to my hips one last time. They buck wildly as we come together, breathing harshly through our noses, muffling each other's pleasure with our lips pressed together, our tongues tasting one another. When our lips part, her laugh is teary, soft.

I brush my thumbs against her cheeks again as she slowly slides back, adjusting our clothes. She laughs at the ruined waistband on her shorts. Spotting the hair tie on the floor, she laughs again as she uses it to secure a knot on her waist band. I'm drained of all energy and just watch. She looks back at me, then smooths her hands down my chest in an attempt to fix my wrinkled shirt.

"I need a minute," she says softly as she leans forward, kissing the corner of my mouth while standing.

Silently, I nod, watching her walk out of the door, closing it gently behind her.

Being left alone was not what I had in mind, and I had hoped to avoid it. My mind races with a flurry of thoughts and endless questions, leaving me restless as I anxiously fidget with the hem of my shirt.

Everything feels out of place–the memories, the awareness of them, and the emotions they are stirring within me. I can't escape the recollections of Sydney before the accident, nor the brief moments we shared recently.

These new memories seem to serve as testaments to the deep bond and lasting affection we once had, but the fact remains unchanged. She had chosen to marry Brad, who happened to be my best friend at that time. I find myself grappling with the question: What had led her to marry Brad if not affection?

After what seems like an eternity, Sydney returns, carrying a tray with a light meal. Her face bears an expression of concern as she sets the tray down beside me on the bench. "I bought you a sandwich and some soup. I've heard it's essential to have something in your stomach after donating blood," she says, surprisingly gentle. It heavily contrasts her spite mere minutes ago.

I muster a weak smile, grateful for her consideration. As I begin eating, she sits across from me, maintaining the silence.

Her demeanor softens as she sighs. "I'm sorry," she apologizes, catching me off guard. "I know it must have been difficult to be unaware of a lot of things, and then I yell at you. I've just been..." she pauses, staring down at her feet.

"Angry," I mumble under my breath, and she nods. "Understandable." Monosyllabic responses are all I can muster right now.

"It wasn't easy, the first year after your accident," she slowly begins. "I got sick and checked in at a clinic, and I found out I was two months pregnant with Damon. Keeping the truth hidden from everyone proved to be hard at first, then Brad figured it out and offered to help. Looking back now, it seems like he may have taken advantage of my vulnerability, but the fact remains that he was there."

"Is that why you married him?" I inquire, wrestling with the bitterness that has taken hold of me. "You fell in love with him?"

My heart pounds with each beat, hoping desperately that she will deny it. The thought of her loving someone else gnaws at my sanity despite the passing of ten years.

"It wasn't out of love," she confesses. "In a way, he rescued me from my parents. You remember how conservative they are. In some ways, more difficult than your mother. I had managed to conceal the pregnancy from them, but when I went into labor, my father took me to the hospital and found out. He outright disowned his own daughter while she was in the middle of labor," she says with a bitter laugh.

I shift my gaze downward, my fists clenched tightly in frustration. Throughout our interactions, I had come to understand that her father was an unreasonable man. Yet I had always believed that, in any situation, he would prioritize his daughter over any trivial matters. However, it is apparent that assumption was wrong.

"Brad stepped in and claimed to be the father. My father immediately ordered him to take responsibility, and within weeks, we were married. Truly, it didn't fully register that I had married him until about six months had passed."

"Then, your parents... did they—"

"No, still an absolute scandal. I was pregnant before I got married. I was supposedly engaged to you and then got pregnant by Brad. Which meant that I cheated on you! Triple scandal! My mother has never met Damon. My father only saw him at birth. They didn't come to the wedding, which was a civil ceremony. Other than Brad, I was completely alone."

As Sydney pours her heart out, sharing her heart-wrenching revelations, I can't escape the overwhelming sense of guilt welling up from within. It is as if I had deserted her that very day when she pleaded with me not to leave. If I had stayed, would it have altered the course of life, leading us all away from such bleak circumstances? Sydney and I could have been married, raising our son together, while my brother and his wife could have raised Katie alongside us.

Addressing Sydney, my voice falters as I hesitate, feeling the weight of remorse. "I'm so sorry for not being there for you when you needed me the most. I can't imagine the pain and loneliness you endured all those years."

Her eyes soften with understanding as she responds, "Gabe, it's not your fault. We are all victims of the situation."

She is right, of course. But we are also victims of my mother's actions. My mother's involvement caused a lot of damage. Although I should not hold my mother responsible for the decisions I made, her interference contributed to the unfortunate distance that arose between Sydney and me. And this led to me ultimately missing the first ten years of my son's life. This situation is hardly acceptable.

Even worse, had I continued with my belief that Sydney and Brad's union was founded on love, I would have remained oblivious to my son's very existence.

Anger swells inside me, bubbling up like a volcano, ready to erupt. I can't contain the frustration and regret that grips my heart. Without thinking, I jump up from the metal bench, the tray of food crashing to the floor, forgotten in the heat of the moment. I dash out of the room, my sole purpose etched firmly in my mind–find Larissa Hartwell, my mother. The urgency of the task propels me forward, igniting urgency in every step I take.

"I can't believe this! I can't believe she kept all this from me for so long!" My voice reverberates with anger as I look around, trying to find my mother. She needs to hear it, the consequences of her actions that are now haunting our lives.

Sydney hurries after me, trying to keep up with my strides. "Gabe, where are you going?"

I storm into the reception area, scanning the crowd for my mother's face. Finally, I spot her near a corner, engaging in animated conversation with her phone pressed against her cheek. The sight of her talking so casually, completely unbothered by the situation while the rest of our lives have been turned upside down, fuels my anger even more.

"Mother!" I yell, pushing through the hospital crowd to reach her. Heads turn with curious gazes following my outburst. "We need to talk, now!" my voice cracks with the overwhelming emotions threatening to engulf me.

My mother turns toward me, her expression shifting from surprise to concern. "Gabe, what's gotten into you?" she asks, attempting to keep her composure as she squares her shoulders.

"What's gotten into me? How about the fact that your meddling and interference have ruined our lives?" I spit out the words, my anger intensifying with every syllable.

Sydney places a hand on my arm, trying to calm me down, but I shrug her off, my focus solely on my mother. "You knew Sydney was trying to make contact, and you let her suffer all those years without saying a word. You ruined our chance to be together, for me to raise my son, and for what? To protect your precious reputation?"

My mother's face pales as she attempts to speak, but I do not grant her the opportunity. "You have no comprehension of the immense pain and heartache you have inflicted upon us! We lost ten years, a decade of happiness, all because you could not bear the thought of me being with someone who did not belong to your social circle."

The people around us have fallen silent, their eyes fixated on the unfolding drama. Sydney tugs at my arm again, urging me to step away from the scene, but I can't contain my pent-up anger any longer.

"You know what, Mom? I don't care about your reputation anymore. You can keep your social status, your fancy parties, and your empty friendships! I'm moving on with my life!" The words burn as they leave my mouth, a mixture of anger and sorrow spilling out like a tidal wave.

Before my mother can respond, I turn away, leaving the intake area, and Sydney trailing close behind me. Once we step outside, seeking refuge from prying eyes, I instinctively pull her close and gently press my face against the warm crevice where her neck meets her shoulder.

"I'm so sorry," I murmur, my voice trembling with emotion, the words partly muffled by her clothes.

"I'm sorry, too," she whispers, her fingers delicately grazing my back. Somehow, the gesture feels like she is conveying a silent reassurance that we are in this together.

And I really hope we are.

CHAPTER 23

Sydney

"Mom, am I going to be okay?" Damon asks, twiddling his thumbs.

"Of course, sweetie. I made sure of it," I reassure him, trying to offer comfort to my young son. Gently, I reach out and envelope his small frame in my arms, being cautious not to apply too much pressure.

The doctors had mentioned that he was weak after the surgery. Though I know a hug can't do much damage, I want to be careful.

It has been three days since I had told Gabe about Damon being his son, and during this time, Gabe has been hovering by Damon's door, hesitant to meet him. As for Damon, he had just woken up from the surgery a day ago, and his recovery is still underway.

Despite the uncertainty surrounding Gabe's presence, I focus on Damon's well-being, knowing that anything could potentially delay his recovery. I sit beside Damon's hospital bed and observe his small, pale face and lank dark hair.

Throughout the long hours I've spent at his bedside, Damon's frail appearance has struck a painful chord within me. His once-vibrant spirit has been temporarily dimmed, worn down by the trials of his injury and the surgery that followed. Despite the medical equipment softly humming around him, the room feels overwhelmingly silent, amplifying the seriousness of his situation. But his appearance is a reminder to me of how important it is to remain strong for him during this challenging time.

Throughout Damon's stay, I've sensed Gabe's internal struggle from his periodic glances through the slightly ajar door. I understand he needs time to process everything, but I also hope he will find the courage to step inside and face his son, as Damon also needs his father's love and support.

Damon releases himself from the hug, fixing his innocent, wide, hazel eyes on me as he inquires, "Mom, who is the man standing at the door?"

I blink in surprise. Gabe's presence hasn't escaped Damon's keen observation. It seems his attempts at subtlety weren't as successful as he had hoped, but then again, Damon has never been one to miss anything.

A sudden idea crosses my mind, and considering all factors, it feels like the right approach.

"He is your blood donor, and apparently, he's feeling a bit shy about coming to say hi," I reply playfully, observing Damon as he turns slightly to glance at the door.

"That's silly. Grown-ups aren't shy," he retorts, his tone surprisingly sassy, eliciting a chuckle from me.

"Oh, they certainly can be," I affirm, nodding with a knowing smile.

"Well, I should say hi then," he asserts, catching my attention with his confident tone. Before I can fully process his words, Damon gently leaps off the bed, his small frame bouncing on the floor as he rushes toward the door.

Instinctively, I lunge to catch hold of his IV pole just before it topples over. "Damon!" I call out in concern. His IV could come out, causing unnecessary setbacks.

Where did he get this unexpected surge of energy? He knows he shouldn't be exerting himself so much.

Amid the sudden high tension, the door bursts open, and Gabe hurries in, managing to intercept Damon just before his IV line strains. "What's wrong?" Gabe inquires, placing both hands on Damon's shoulders to steady him while his eyes carefully scan the small boy's frame.

At least he is over his shyness.

"Damon, you can't simply jump out of bed like that," I exclaim, relieved that Damon is unharmed. I gently reposition his IV pole before joining them both. "The doctor said you should stay in bed as much as possible."

"But I just wanted to say hi," Damon explains with innocent enthusiasm. It is clear that his intentions were good, but his health has to come first.

Understanding Damon's desire to greet Gabe, I soften my tone. "Of course, you want to say hi, and that's sweet, but you must be careful. Now, get back in bed."

Gabe's face breaks into a wide grin, and he points a finger at himself, asking, "You wanted to say hi to me?"

Damon responds with a nod toward Gabe, seemingly disregarding my words. "Yeah, and wow, you're tall for a shy person."

I observe their interaction with keen interest, recognizing that I am unintentionally intruding on their heartfelt meeting. I decide to provide them with some space. Given how attentive and caring he has been with Katie, Gabe will take excellent care of him.

Besides, it is high time I request the DNA test results for Larissa.

Ever since Gabe confronted her, Larissa has been remarkably patient and composed. It must have been quite uncomfortable for her to be put on the spot by her own son. Reflecting on her situation, I resolve to learn from her mistakes and ensure I never repeat them with Damon.

My approach with Damon will be different. I firmly believe in allowing him the freedom to love whomever he chooses, regardless of their social status. Interfering in his life, as Larissa did with Gabe, is something I know I will never do. My past experiences have taught me the pain such interference can cause, and I am determined to never subject Damon to the same ordeal.

"Damon, why don't you keep him company? I'll go get you a snack," I say casually, shooting a glance at Gabe, hoping he understands my intentions. I want him to spend some quality time with his son.

"Sure, Mom. So, what's your name? I'm Damon," he says with excitement, taking small steps toward the hospital bed.

"I'm Gabriel, but you can call me Gabe," Gabe replies, his grin widening as he follows Damon's lead. The atmosphere seems to lighten, and I feel hopeful about the new bond forming between them.

With Damon and Gabe engaged in conversation, I seize the opportunity to step out of the room, leaving their chatting to fade into the background.

As I walk down the hospital's corridors, I can't shake the concern in my heart at Larissa's presence. It has been gnawing at me ever since Gabe confronted her. She could be up to something. It is crucial to find her and the DNA test results.

My steps quicken as I make my way to the hospital cafeteria.

I keep my eyes peeled for any sign of Larissa, hoping she might be seeking a moment of solace amid the bustling hospital cafeteria. But then again, is she the type to be caught eating cafeteria food?

As I approach a stand in the cafeteria, my eyes catch a glimpse of her familiar figure, but it turns out to be false hope. It is just a nurse with a striking resemblance to Larissa. Disappointment washes over me, but I can't afford to give up just yet. I purchase a granola bar for Damon, knowing he will appreciate it.

Back in the hospital corridor, I retrace my steps, my thoughts swirling with the urgency of finding Larissa. Where could she be? Why is she so quiet? It's unnerving.

As I near Damon's room, my eyes dart around, hoping to spot any trace of her. Then, a poised movement catches my attention. There she is, standing at a distance, engaged in conversation with a doctor. Relief washes over me at the sight of her. I approach them, clutching the granola bar.

Just as I am about to call out to her, I see the doctor handing her a letter, and Larissa's expression shifts from boredom to subtle cynicism. My curiosity piques, and I stop a few steps away, trying to gauge what their exchange is about.

My heart pounds relentlessly, invaded by a wild and unsettling thought. Is it possible that Larissa, harboring ill intentions, has falsified the results to show a negative outcome just to crush my spirit? Moreover, I can't shake the nagging fear that she might also deny Damon solely because he is my son.

Yet, before allowing myself to plunge into despair, I realize I need to take action. I can't simply stand by and let doubt consume me. Instead, I resolve to face the situation head-on. Larissa needs to be confronted about the legitimacy of the results.

I turn on my feet and stride purposefully to the nurse's desk to inquire about the test results. To my relief, the same nurse is there, and her somewhat familiar face instantly puts me at ease, a comfort I had not anticipated but am grateful for.

"Good afternoon," I greet her with a polite smile. "I'm here to check on the DNA test results that I requested."

"Mrs. Romero, right?" the nurse asks, her fingers tapping swiftly on the keyboard in front of her. "The results have just come in, and Mrs. Hartwell most likely received a copy of it."

"Did she now?" I murmur, drawing out the words with a hint of skepticism.

As if on cue, the conversation is interrupted by the whirring of a printer. The nurse deftly reaches below her desk, retrieving a warm, thin paper, which she hands to me with a gentle smile. The crisp sheet bears the test results.

Glancing down at the paper, I can feel my heart quicken with anticipation. The results are laid out clearly, and as I skim through them, a sense of relief washes over me. Everything appears to be in order.

The confirmation of Gabe being Damon's father is stated with clarity.

"Thank you," I express my gratitude to the receptionist before calmly retracing my steps back to Gabe and Damon. I have an inkling Larissa will be with them.

Upon reaching the hallway that leads to the room, I notice Gabe and Larissa deeply engrossed in conversation. A pronounced furrow marks Gabe's forehead while Larissa has her back turned to me; her attire and the sleek bun atop her head are unmistakably familiar.

My immediate concern is for Damon—is he alright? I quicken my pace, and as I approach them, Gabe's gaze shifts toward me, prompting a sharp glare from my end. Someone should be with Damon!

"Sydney," Gabe's expression softens, a sight that tugs at my heart, but I forcefully push aside any emotions.

"You left him alone?" my question slips out, unintentionally carrying a hint of spite.

Before Gabe has a chance to respond, I hurry into the room, desperate to ensure Damon's well-being. To my surprise, the space is occupied by a team of doctors and nurses.

Panic engulfs me. Did something happen to him?

"Damon?" I whisper, my voice barely audible, as the mere thought of something happening to him sends shivers down my spine. The room is teeming with people, making it impossible for me to catch a glimpse of him amid the crowd.

Are things that serious?

"Relax, Sydney. I'm having him moved to a better room," Larissa interrupts, her voice carrying an oddly monotone quality, cutting through the horrid thoughts running through my mind. "He's my grandson, after all... and a Hartwell heir," she adds as if that would bring reassurance.

Confusion sets in, and I turn to look at her. "What?"

"You heard me, right? Or were the results lying?"

CHAPTER 24

Sydney

The move to the new room happens swiftly, and Damon seems to relish the experience as he is gently pushed in a wheelchair through the hospital hallways.

Following Larissa's request, I left Damon in the room with her. Larissa appeared sincere, without any hidden motives, as she genuinely sought to connect with her grandson.

Beyond her typical apathy, Larissa has revealed herself as a reasonable woman who ultimately cares deeply for her family, always desiring the best for them. This became evident when she had Damon moved to a private room with access to top-notch doctors.

I was surprised by the gesture, as I hadn't known such arrangements were possible, but Larissa managed it, all for Damon's well-being.

Upon encountering Gabe, he told me he had admonished his mother for requesting the room change without my consent. It was gratifying that he was supporting my perspective on the matter. I owe him an apology for hastily assuming that he had left our son unattended.

Coincidentally, just as these thoughts crossed my mind, a warm breath brushes against the skin of my cheek and neck, and Gabe's cool voice inquires, "What's on your mind?"

"You," I say honestly, stepping back from the door to Damon's new room. With a few decisive strides, I settle onto one of the maroon couches that are thoughtfully arranged in his waiting room. This side of the hospital is definitely posh in every aspect.

Gabe follows suit and sits beside me, his words flowing hesitantly as he jokes lightly, "What part of me are you thinking about?"

His green eyes bore into mine, full of mischief, as I shoot him a look. Despite everything, he remains resilient in his humor. Unable to suppress it any longer, my chest shakes with laughter.

"I'm being serious," I insist, playfully shoving him.

He retorts smoothly, "So am I." His mouth moves ever so slightly.

I let my gaze linger on his lips, noting their curve. Given everything that has happened recently, I am unsure if Gabe truly has any romantic feelings for me. Or any relationship that involves just the two of us. It's understandable if he feels some resentment towards me. I married his best friend and kept the knowledge of his son from him. It weighs heavily on my mind.

"Sydney," Gabe beckons, his voice a gentle caress as he pronounces my name.

His tenderness evokes a gentle thump in my chest. I turn to look at him, the flutter of his long lashes guarding the depths of his emerald eyes, his artfully stubbled cheeks, and the subtle parting of his lips.

"Yeah?" I whisper, my heart rate increasing as he inches closer to my face. His proximity sends a wave of warmth through me, and I swallow, trying to compose myself.

As Gabe's fingers gently stroke my cheek, he offers a warm smile, his eyes reflecting mine. "Don't worry so much. I'm here now."

Hearing his words, for a moment, I forget the complexities that surround us. His presence alone has alleviated my apprehensions. But hearing the reassurance in his words, my affection for him swells, and I find myself drawing closer to him.

His fingers slide from my cheek, around to the back of my neck, the tips of them curling against me, into my hair, and my breath catches. When his lips ghost across mine, my heart skips a beat.

"Gabe," I breathe out his name softly, and he deepens the kiss slowly, stirring the heat to life in my lower stomach.

Brushing my tongue against his as it asks for permission at the seam of my lips, I lean into his chest, fingers splayed against his shirt. My heart is pounding an aching emotional beat that risks feeling overwhelming.

He's here now, with me.

I slide my hands up to his shoulders as he presses against me, arms curling around my waist to hold me closer.

Coming up for air, I'm lost in his eyes as he smiles softly at me, and a sharp, cold voice breaks the tender moment. "Sydney." Larissa's voice reaches me, and I pull away from Gabe with a slight blush tinting my cheeks.

How embarrassing. Hopefully, she won't use our short romantic moment against us.

Larissa enters the waiting area with slow, calculated steps. "Damon is asking for you," she informs me, her eyes burrowing into my frame.

If she enjoyed her conversation with my son, she is doing an exceptional job concealing her feelings.

I nod, my heart still fluttering from the kiss that just happened. As I shoot up from the couch, Larissa and I exchange glares. The judgment in her eyes reverberates loudly, yet my determination to remain steady prevails. She holds little significance to me.

As I observe her, it is clear she remains unchanged from the person I once knew. I find comfort in her consistency, though. It would be unsettling if she were to suddenly show affection merely because I happen to be the mother of her only grandson. Her cold demeanor seems unyielding, unaffected by our familial connection.

I turn away from her with a composed smile plastered on my face and enter Damon's room. He is now lying in a wider hospital bed with an abundance of cream sheets and fluffy blankets, his eyes brightening as I walk in. "Mom!" he exclaims, his small voice full of excitement.

How does he always seem to have more than enough energy?

I settle by his side and lean to hug him gently, feeling the warmth of his embrace. "Hey, sweetie," I respond, my heart aching at the innocence in his eyes.

Damon looks over at the door before quietly asking. "Who are they, Mom?"

What do I tell him? He has grown up with the firm belief that Brad is his father. The mere thought of revealing a different truth fills me with trepidation. I know it could potentially shatter the world he has known his whole life.

I hesitate, struggling to find the right words. "Well, that man is a very special friend," I say, careful with my phrasing. "And the old lady, she's like a grandmother to you, Damon."

His eyes widen in wonder. "Like a grandma?" he questions, skepticism coloring his tone.

"Yes, kind of like that," I reply, knowing this explanation only scratches the surface of the truth.

Damon continues to ask more questions, his innocent curiosity both heartwarming and challenging. I do my best to answer truthfully while protecting him from the complexities of his evolving family situation. It is not an easy task, and I can only hope that someday, he will understand everything more clearly.

Damon suddenly yells, "Dad!"

The unexpected outburst triggers a violent thumping in my chest. My heart races as I swiftly turn to see who he is calling for. To my surprise, standing just inside the doorway is Brad, my ex-husband. Gabe is standing behind him, his expression serious and silent.

"What are you doing here?" I question, attempting to filter the irritation. Damon is here, after all. "I didn't expect you to show up."

Brad seems taken aback by my question and quickly explains, "I just got your message when I got back from my trip. I came as soon as I could."

"Well, you're late," I reply tersely, unable to hide the disappointment in my voice.

Brad shoots a side glance at Gabe. "I know." Then, he turns his attention back to me and asks, "Can I spend some time with Damon?"

"Yeah! Can he?" Damon clasps my arm, his enthusiasm painted across his small face.

How can I ever refuse that?

I hesitate for a moment, realizing there are many unresolved issues between us that need to be addressed. "We have a lot to discuss," I reply, looking at Gabe, who gives me a reassuring nod.

I take a deep breath and continue, "But yes, you can spend some time with Damon."

After leaving Damon alone in the room with Brad, I make my way out to the hospital corridor, distancing myself from the confined environment. I continue walking and soon find myself stepping outside, greeted by a gust of refreshing air that fills my lungs.

The sun is slowly setting, casting warm hues of gold and orange through the windows. I take another deep breath, feeling the cool air refresh my senses after the emotional rollercoaster of the past few days.

Gabe walks beside me, his hands buried in the pockets of his black pants. We walk silently for a while, our footsteps the only audible sound—the weight of unspoken words hanging in the air like a thick fog.

Finally, breaking the silence, Gabe gently inquires, "What happened between you and Brad? I mean, I know about the divorce, but I want to know what led to it. I mean, it feels odd; you're clearly uncomfortable around him."

I exhale deeply, humming before I think about my recent years with Brad. "Brad," I pause, "Brad and I had our fair share of happy moments during our marriage," I begin, recollecting the times we got close to having a small romantic relationship.

"But there were also moments of hurt on my side, more actually seeing as no matter how much time we spent, I was never able to love him as passionately as I did you." I look at Gabe with a small smile before continuing. "It got bad when he cheated on me. I think I told you that back at the estate. And that shattered the trust we had built over the years. The divorce two years ago was rough, but we both needed to find our own paths."

Gabe listens attentively, his expression colored with genuine concern. "I'm sorry you had to go through all that."

"It's fine. It's all in the past now," I breathe softly, shaking off the weight of my memories with Brad. "What matters most is moving forward and focusing on Damon's well-being."

Gabe suddenly halts his steps to face me, his eyes searching mine. "Sydney, I would never hurt you like that," he utters earnestly. "Give me a chance, and I promise I'll cherish you and Damon with all my heart."

His words resonate deeply within me, stirring emotions I never knew were present. Until this moment, I had assumed he preferred to maintain some distance and never imagined that he would want to be completely involved in both of our lives. The revelation is truly heartwarming, an unexpected ray of light warming my heart.

"Gabe," I whisper.

He reaches out, gently taking my hand in his. "You don't have to tell me anything now. Take all the time you need."

The trees' rustling grows loud, the sun's warm glow feels more prominent, and the air around us becomes charged with emotion. I feel torn between the past and the present, between the hurt I've experienced and the hope that Gabe is offering.

"I just want you to know that I love you, Sydney, and ten years of memory loss did nothing to change that. I love you." He pulls me into an embrace. I feel his large arms wrap around me as he pulls me closer to his taller frame.

"And I plan to for the next ten years, twenty, too, and fifty, if we live that long. Life hasn't been complete without you, and I would rather lose myself than live like that again."

Immediately, a profound sense of certainty envelopes me, eradicating any trace of doubt that may have been lingering. The powerful undercurrent of passion, which has been simmering between us, finally takes control, guiding us toward an inevitable connection.

As our lips gently brush against each other, an electric current surges through my entire being, igniting a fervent fire within that I can no longer suppress. It is a kiss that transcends time, leaving an indelible mark on my soul.

Under the soft glow of the fading sunlight, we find ourselves intertwined in each other's arms, seemingly suspended in a timeless embrace. Every gesture, every touch, speaks volumes without the need for words. The world around us disappears into insignificance, and all that matters is the connection we share.

As the sun sets, painting the sky with hues of pink and purple, our kiss deepens, and it feels like coming home. I stop feeling lost in the complexities of my past. I can only feel Gabe and the way to a future for both of us where love and hope intertwine.

Hopefully, I am ready to take that chance.

The walk back to Damon's room is filled with hand-holding and light waves of laughter as we talk. However, our moment of joy is harshly interrupted by the concerned expression on Larissa's face as she stands with security officers by Damon's door.

Damon!

CHAPTER 25

Gabriel

"Damon is missing," my mother reveals, her voice colored with a chilling tone that unsettles me. "And so is Brad," she adds.

Initially, I find myself entertaining the notion that she might be joking, though this skepticism swiftly gives way to an overwhelming sense of dread. The idea of my once close friend kidnapping my son is unsettling beyond words.

Sydney has completely lost control. Lashing out angrily at the innocent security officers who are merely doing their job. Despite the temptation to correct her, I refrain from pointing out that, technically, it can't be called kidnapping, as Brad does identify as Damon's father, and Damon still believes that to be true.

That sharp, bitter sting in my chest returns once more prompting me to let her be. The idea that Brad has been living the role that I feel should have been mine leaves me feeling disgusted and angry. He had once been my closest confidant, and to this day, the memories of our friendship retain a remarkable, vivid quality, even though years have elapsed.

It seems like only yesterday when I had entrusted Brad watching out for Sydney before I departed a week in L.A., and now, a decade has slipped away. In that time, not only did he marry her, but he also raised my son alongside her.

And now, I'm standing in the security room of a hospital, watching security footage from cameras outside Damon's room observing intently as the footage shows Brad cautiously poking his head out of Damon's room and glancing around before eventually stepping out. Much to my dismay, Damon follows suit, mimicking Brad's actions and emerging from the room.

Hand in hand, they both stroll out of the camera's view. I could continue watching the remaining videos to trace their path and the route they took, but it is too painful to watch.

Damon seems genuinely thrilled to be trailing after Brad.

With a sense of disbelief, I tear my eyes away from the glowing screen. "Where on earth would he take Damon, do you think?" I fight the panic that is building inside me. Already, I feel protective over my son.

Sydney impatiently brushes tears from her cheek. "We used to share our location on our phones when Damon was little, just in case something went wrong. That way, we'd know where the other had last been." Her hand trembles slightly as she opens the location tracking app. "Here! I see where his phone is, so it's likely where they are, too!"

I glance over her shoulder, seeing a large square of green on the map. "A park?"

Sydney nods. "It seems so. I can't believe he would just take him. Anything he needed to say to him, he could have said here, where Damon was safe."

"He needs to pay for what he's done, endangering my son," I grit out.

Sydney's objection is immediate, and she steps forward, her moist face contorting with worry as she places a calming hand on my arm. "Damon still thinks of Brad as his father. Let's at least try to give him the benefit of the doubt for now."

Her plea strikes me hard, and I feel a surge of bitterness blending with understanding. It is true. Damon has formed a bond with Brad, and ripping that connection apart could indeed cause lasting damage. He might even grow to hate me if he finds out I interfered with his relationship with the only dad he'd ever known. Reluctantly, I acknowledge Sydney's concern.

Overwhelmed with the weight of my emotions and the situation on my shoulders, I move to leave the security room, but as I do, my knee gives way, causing me to stumble. Pain shoots through my leg, a reminder of my limits, my past, my pain.

My knee had to choose this inopportune moment to act up as if to remind me of my shortcomings. Throughout my life, it seems that I only excel in one thing: losing the people I love. If only I had been a better version of myself, perhaps all the heartache and pain could have been averted.

Brad would have never ended up marrying Sydney. I could have been the one raising Damon, becoming the reliable figure with whom Damon would willingly entrust everything. Our bond would have been unbreakable, and I would have been a pillar of support for him.

Sydney is by my side in an instant, steadying me with concern painted on her face. "Easy Gabe," she urges, worry evident in her voice. "You're pushing yourself too hard."

I manage a faint smile, touched by her concern. "I'll be fine," I assure her, though deep down, I can feel my resolve teetering. With a deep breath, I steel myself for the challenges ahead. Brad has taken my son, and despite my personal feelings, I have to ensure Damon's safety and well-being.

How ironic, Brad, once my best friend, has become a stranger, and now I have to confront the consequences of his actions.

As Sydney leads me out of the security room, my mind churns with emotions. I try to maintain my composure, but the weight of the situation is crushing me. The fear for Damon's safety, the frustration of my past mistakes, and the anger at Brad's reckless actions are all taking their toll.

As we walk down the brightly lit corridor, I feel the urge to cry, to let out the pent-up emotions that have been building inside me. I stumble slightly, and Sydney steadies me. She knows me so well, and it is both comforting and painful to have her by my side.

She doesn't deserve any of this. None of it.

Unable to hold back any longer, I break down, burying my face in her shoulder as tears stream down my face. "I'm so sorry, Sydney," I choke out between sobs. "I'm sorry for everything you've been through because of me."

"Gabe." Sydney holds me tightly, her arms a comforting embrace. "It's not your fault," she whispers, her voice gentle and soothing. "None of this is your fault."

But I can't help but feel responsible. If I had been there for Damon from the beginning, if I had been there for her, maybe none of this would have happened. Maybe Damon wouldn't have been taken, and Sydney wouldn't have had to endure all this.

"I should have been there for you," I mumble, my voice barely audible. "I should have been there for Damon."

Sydney gently lifts my face, her eyes filled with compassion. "You've done nothing but support us since you found us, Gabe," she says firmly. "You've been there for Damon in so many ways already. You saved his life, for God's sake. And as for Brad, his choices are his own. You can't blame yourself for that."

Her words offer some comfort, but the pain in my heart is still raw. "I just want Damon to be safe," I say, my voice trembling. "I can't bear the thought of anything happening to him."

Sydney wipes away my tears, her touch gentle and reassuring. "We will go get him," she says, her voice determined. "And we'll make sure he's safe."

Her strength gives me hope, and I cling to it desperately. We continue walking, Sydney supporting me both physically and emotionally. She guides me to sit on a nearby bench. Everything in me wants to run out the door like a wild man and confront Brad Romero, but she is right. I need a moment to rest my knee, and despite her anger, Sydney seems to believe Brad wouldn't outright harm Damon.

"I know this is difficult for you," she says softly, sitting beside me. "But we'll get through this together. Damon is strong, and he has you as his father. We'll bring him back, I promise."

I stretch my leg a few more times and then nod to Sydney. "I'm ready."

Sydney and I waste no time. We rush out of the hospital, navigating through the crowd of people and cars on our way. The tension is palpable as we search for my car amid the chaos.

"There it is!" Sydney points at the familiar sleek black vehicle, and I quickly unlock the car, both of us hopping inside. I rev the engine, and we speed off toward the park.

Sydney holds my hand with a firm grip as I drive, pushing the car to its limits, my mind abuzz with countless potential scenarios. I am confused by Brad's actions and am hopeful his decision to remove Damon from the hospital isn't hurting my son's health. Now that I am calmer, I know Brad wouldn't purposefully hurt him. He had assumed the role of Damon's father.

As we arrive, we see a group of people gathered near a playground. Among them, I spot Brad and Damon sitting on a bench, eating ice cream. Damon seems joyful even as he is still clad in his hospital clothes, laughing at something Brad said. My heart swells at the sight of my son, safe and happy. But the thought of everything that has happened weighs heavily on me.

I park the car, and we both rush toward them. It is hard to navigate through the crowd while keeping my focus on the two of them, watching as they switch to more serious demeanors.

As we approach from their side, I overhear Damon speaking to Brad.

"Since the divorce," Damon says, his voice surprisingly calm.

Brad looks taken aback and asks gently, "How?"

"You said it. *Just because we aren't related doesn't mean you can take him away from me, Sydney,*" Damon quotes, faking a deep voice.

Is he trying to mimic Brad?

Sydney gasps in shock, and I struggle to grasp the weight of his words, but an idea tickles my mind. Sydney and I stand there, feeling like intruders in this intimate moment between Damon and Brad. The bond they share is evident, and it tears at my heart.

Damon turns to Brad and asks, "Do you know him? My real dad?"

It is then that I understand. Damon has been aware all along that Brad isn't his actual father. He has known all along. Fear grips me as I contemplate a reality where Damon might believe his biological father to be a terrible person.

"Yeah, he's not a good man. He tricked your mom into loving him and left her alone when he found out she was pregnant,"

Brad asserts, his tone filled with malice that I have never really recognized before.

My chest thumps against my ribcage violently as I realize Brad's intentions. He is trying to manipulate Damon.

I am about to step in, but Damon's small voice speaks up, surprising me.

"That's a lie. I've read Mommy's journals. He doesn't remember me," Damon pushes back, jumping out of his seat and facing Brad. His small face contorted by anger.

"Why would I lie to you, Damon?" Brad drawls.

"That's enough!" Sydney cuts in, surprising all of us. I hadn't even noticed when she left my side and approached them.

Brad jumps up, looking like a deer caught in headlights. "S-Sydney," he stammers.

"I trusted you with my life, my son's life, and all this time, your intentions were only ever to manipulate me and my son?"

"No, I wasn't—" His words halt as he catches sight of me. "You, this is all you," he accuses, and Damon flinches.

"Sydney, take Damon away," I firmly order, and she nods immediately.

"Come, honey, we have a lot to talk about," she whispers gently to Damon.

"No, wait." Brad shifts to reach them, but I intercept him, shoving him back.

When I'm sure they are out of the immediate area, I walk up to Brad, hoping he will feel my exact intentions when his jaw meets my fist.

Epilogue

Sydney

It's mind-blowing to think that just a few months ago, I pretended to be someone else to secure funding for my clinic. Little did I realize that impulsive decision would pave the way for the newfound life I now share with Gabe.

We're at UTC Ice Sports. We have an entire rink to ourselves thanks to Gabe. Damon is playing with Gabe on the ice. He's recently becoming more accepting of Gabe being his father.

After the unfortunate incident with Brad, I realized I needed to tell Damon the truth immediately. At first, he was slightly wary of Gabe. I was afraid that Brad had successfully convinced him that his father was a terrible person. However, Damon's curiosity got the better of him, and he was receptive to spending some time with Gabe, which led to a shift in his feelings, albeit slower than I expected.

About a month after Damon's release from hospital, I found him sitting alone, hunched, with a sad, downcast expression on his face.

"Damon, hon. What's the matter?"

Tears start streaming down his face. Alarmed, I put my arm around him. "Are you hurt? What's wrong?"

A few more sobs and he buries his head in my shoulder. "M-mom... I really like Gabe. I don't want him to lose his memory again... f-forget me again. I don't know what to do to make him not forget me."

His admission jolts me in a bizarre way. While his fear devastates me, his desire to be with Gabe brings me relief and joy.

After many conversations with Gabe about why such a thing was not likely to happen again, Damon's reluctance to open up to Gabe melted away.

They've also bonded over skating, and now hockey. Gabe asked Damon if he wanted to learn to skate, and Damon's eager response delighted Gabe. To my surprise, Damon has taken to skating quite naturally, enjoys his lessons with Gabe, and now wants to learn to play hockey. He had previously shown greater enthusiasm for football.

Damon has also charmed Larissa, who is now eager to actively shape another Hartwell heir. For Damon's sake, I am trying to find it in my heart to forgive her. It is not in Larissa's nature to apologize. But her attitude has thawed slightly and we are making guarded progress.

Gabe continues his therapy sessions, now with the genuine Sara Jensen. His progress has been quite remarkable. Today, before playing with Damon, he completed own his intense workout laps in the empty rink without a single grimace. Damon watched in awe, as did I, but for different reasons.

In his therapy sessions, Gabe honestly acknowledged his longing to get back into skating and hockey. When Sara asked about competing for a spot in the NHL, he admitted he had decided against it. "Skating and hockey are in but I think my glory days in *pro* hockey are behind me. It makes no sense to dwell on the past. Besides, it's much more thrilling and fulfilling to dedicate myself to my family... after all, I've lost 10 years with them and I don't want to lose another minute."

We are having a fun family afternoon at the rink. Katie and I are taking skating lessons, but right now, we're taking a break from our own practice drills and just watching from the players' box. Damon has learned to skate much faster than Katie, and he now skates with a hockey stick. He makes a clumsy yet determined swing, sending the puck wobbling into the net.

"He scores!" Katie exclaims.

"Yes, he did!"

In that moment, witnessing Gabe and Damon's joyous interaction and shared triumph, I can't imagine being any happier. If I had known this is how it would be, I would have tried harder to find a way past Larissa's walls to get to Gabe. But, like Gabe, I don't want to dwell on the past anymore.

I want to simply be here. Away from Brad's ludicrous custody lawsuit, away from Larissa's occasionally insensitive comments, and even away from the stress of orchestrating PTX's expansion. I'll be stepping back from the day to day operations once the expanded clinic is running, but for now, I want to see it finished.

"Sydney, Katie, come back on the ice," Gabe beckons, his loud, deep voice echoing through the empty arena.

Eager to join in on the fun, Katie and I head to the players' box door.

I watch Gabe and Damon as they both gracefully glide over the ice towards us. It's funny how their gliding stance is almost perfectly mirrored. Genetics again or is Damon emulating Gabe that closely?

As we take the last few steps towards the ice, he extends a welcoming hand toward me, suggesting, "Let's do some laps."

Hand in hand, we glide alongside each other as the cool air gently kisses our faces. With a surreal atmosphere created by the arena lights, the rink becomes a magical place that enhances the happiness within us.

Gabe suddenly breaks away from Damon's side and gracefully swirls around me, a mischievous smile on his lips. He extends his hand to me with a theatrical flourish, prompting a laugh to escape my lips.

"May I have this dance?" he asks, his deep emerald eyes shining with affection.

"You may," I reply with a twinkle in my eye, lightly placing my hand in his.

We glide together, moving in sync, our bodies swaying to the unspoken rhythm of our hearts. It feels as if time has slowed down, allowing us to savor every moment of this enchanting experience.

As we skate, Damon and Katie join in, forming a circle on the ice, and we all take turns leading the dance. The laughter and joy echo through the empty stadium, filling the air with warmth and love.

In a moment of lighthearted playfulness, Gabe pretends to stumble, dramatically grabbing onto my hand for support. "Careful there," he teases, chuckling. "You wouldn't want the new CEO of Hartwell Enterprises to get injured, would you?"

I laugh heartily before playing along, giving him a playful push. "Oh, I wouldn't want the new CEO to lose his edge. Your dad would not be happy to have to reverse his early retirement. And your mother... your mother might think I'm trying to get rid of you, gold digger that I am!"

He laughs heartily, his eyes gleaming with affection. "Well, I'm not worried about that. I love you, Sydney, and that's all that matters. Will you do me the honor of being my wife?"

My heart skips a beat as he gets down on one knee, right there on the ice. In that electric moment, the world seems to recede into the background, leaving behind only the intimate connection between Gabe and me.

Overflowing with emotion, I answer softly, "Yes, Gabe." I struggle to steady my trembling voice. "I would be deeply honored to become your wife." Those words carry a promise of a lifetime commitment, forever intertwining our hearts and souls.

With a gentle yet confident touch, he slips a dazzling ring onto my finger, and as I hold it up to the light, the brilliance of the diamond captivates me. It shines like a beacon of hope, symbolizing the radiant future that awaits us as a united family. The intricate details of the ring speak to the care and thoughtfulness with which Gabe has chosen this token of his love.

Katie and Damon, witnessing the exchange, cheer excitedly, their smiles mirroring the joy in our hearts. As they glide closer, with a playful glint in his eye that matches his father's, Damon remarks, "You owe me five bucks. I told you they'd get engaged before the end of the week!" His arm extends toward Katie, a triumphant smile gracing his lips.

Blinking in astonishment, I observe their interaction. Apparently, they had made a bet about the timing of our engagement.

Katie pouts. "Fine, you were right this time," she concedes, reluctantly retrieving a few bills from her pocket and handing them to him. "But don't get too confident. It was just a lucky guess."

Damon turns toward me, a warm smile spreading across his face. "Congratulations, Mom," he quipped playfully, his tone light and jesting, "but please don't make any more babies!"

Gabe bursts into laughter, struggling to get his words out amid the amusement. "No promises there," he says, reaching over to ruffle Damon's hair affectionately.

Seeing Damon's adorable pout, I can't help but smile at the sight of my beloved family gathered together like this. With the weight of the ring on my finger, a rush of emotions overwhelms me, feelings that seem impossible to put into words.

Despite all the challenges and pain we have endured, this moment makes it all worthwhile.

I hope we remain like this forever.

THE END

If you loved *Damaged Billionaire's Surprise Heir*, you will love ***Damaged Bad Boy Billionaire***.

Scan this QR code to visit the Amazon Kindle page for *Damaged Bad Boy Billionaire*

Read chapter one of Allyson and Zander's story,
Damaged Bad Boy Billionaire,
on the very next page!

Damaged Bad Boy Billionaire Sneak Peek

My daughter Hayley is buzzing with excitement.
We're on tour with a hot billionaire race car driver
... and he doesn't know *she's his daughter*.

Two steamy months ended when he disappeared.
My world shattered when I realized I was pregnant.
All calls to him went unanswered.

Fifteen years later, Zander Rhodes walks into my clinic.
Injured but not weak, his shaved head and tatts scream power.

He's a storm of desire wrapped in a racing jacket.
Half-naked in my exam room, his gym-sculpted body turns my
knees to jelly.

I don't want him in my life.
Touring as his team's physio is a no-go.
But his offer to fund my dream treatment center is too enticing.

On tour, tension is high on and off the track.

He doesn't deserve a second chance.
His touch challenges my resolve.
The heat between us ignites the whole circuit.

It's time to tell him the truth about Hayley.

I fear we may be destined to crash and burn—*again*.

———ele———

Chapter 1

Zander

It's the scent of burnt rubber against asphalt. The squeal of tires around a tight corner and the heat visibly rising off the sun-drenched track. I take a deep breath and accept the chaos of it, flooding my bones with that sense of relaxation I don't get anywhere else.

"His time's improving."

I turn to my left to spot Reiner Beck, one of the race engineers. He gives a tight nod at his stopwatch.

"Down two seconds this lap."

I grunt in response and look at the track as Jesse comes squealing around the corner, too loose and messy. I click my tongue against my teeth as Reiner sighs and throws the stopwatch on the desk in front of us.

"He gets too ahead of 'imself," Reiner sighs, easing into an oil-stained chair. I signal for the lights to change so Jesse will join us.

"He's a kid. He'll grow out of it."

"He'd better," he grumbles. "He's your kid."

I don't correct him as Jesse comes jogging towards us, his helmet in his arms, a giant grin on his face. "Spun out a little at the end there, I *know*, but my time was down, right?"

I exhale loudly. "Time down means nothing if you're all over the place." I give a curt nod at the car. "Bring it in. We'll talk."

Jesse scowls, but he spins on his heel to go get the car.

Reiner raises his eyebrows. "You gon' let him get away with a bad lap like that?"

"Absolutely not. He's a kid, but he has to learn somehow."

Jesse groans with all the power a sixteen-year-old can possess when he sees me standing by the car with a tub of polish and a toothbrush.

"Come on, Uncle Zander," he says, his shoulders slumping forward. "Look, I was a little off my game today. I get it, but I'll be late for school if I do that, and isn't school important?"

I narrow my eyes. "Not if you're quick about it. You clearly don't know how the car works if you treat it like that. Get to work. You have an hour. Stay clean. You don't want to be late for school after all. School is very important."

I hand him the toothbrush, pat him on the shoulder, and limp towards the garage office.

I rub my leg as I gingerly sit in the squeaky old office chair before sighing at the notification on my phone.

Appointment at Elite Sports Physio–9:30am

I grimace and shove my phone on the desk. What's one more physical therapist to say they've run out of options? What's one more arrogant son-of-a-bitch that thinks they know the exact cure right away only to be proven wrong when I continue to have the same problem day after day?

I get my phone back and look at Elite Sports Physio's website–the latest clinic my dad has set up.

Blah, blah, blah, *we work with athletes*, blah, blah, *we know the body*, blah.

I scroll through the list of employees, and my heart suddenly stops for half a second as I sit up straight.

Allyson Peters, PT, owner.

Allyson Peters.

Fuck, she looks better than when I saw her last. She'd been thin and wiry in college, her long legs built for the track-and-field team. She could outrun me easily. The photo on the website is only a headshot, but she looks great. Her hair is a lighter blonde than I remember, but she seems calm and content. It has to be, *God*, almost fifteen years since I saw her last, just another in a string of people I've loved and left too early.

I purse my lips and decide maybe the appointment would bring some relief after all–just not exactly what my dad intended when he set it up.

"We'll need you back at the racetrack this afternoon," I say as I pull up in front of Jesse's school. He won't be my responsibility for a blissful few hours, although, comparatively, he's a pretty good kid. I hadn't expected to be a sudden dad or a dad at all. In fact, I'd actively fought *against* being a dad, but at least Jess makes it easy.

"I know, I know."

"We've got a tour coming up. Need you top of your game, okay?"

He gives me a calm grin. "Yeah, I know. It's been drilled into my head. I'll get a ride there. Don't worry about me!" He launches himself out of the car and races towards a group of guys waiting by the school doors. I only recognize one of the guys as Roland, his best friend since elementary school.

I do feel bad that I didn't pay much attention to my nephew as he was growing up. It was only when he was suddenly in my care at the age of twelve that I had to do a crash course in how to parent a pre-teen. A grieving one at that.

As Jesse disappears into the school building, a mess of teenage hormones and pranks, I drive toward Allyson Peters' physical therapy clinic. It's close to an hour away from Anaheim, but if she can do something, I'll gladly make that trip.

I'm halfway through the trip when my phone starts ringing through the car. "Tanner, what do you need?"

My assistant's chirpy, sometimes-irritating voice sounds through my car at a volume I wasn't ready for. "Good morning, Mr. Rhodes!"

I scowl as I get stuck in even more L.A. traffic. At this rate, it'll be a whole extra hour to get to Santa Monica. "Yeah, yeah, get to it. I've got a—"

"The appointment at Elite Sports Physio. I'm aware. I was A, checking that you were on the way, and B, letting you know that Dawn Rillerton from the Bradford Beer Company is going to call in five minutes to discuss sponsorship details."

"Ah. Thank—"

"Have a good day, Mr. Rhodes! What time do you think you'll arrive at the garage today?"

"At this rate? Tomorrow."

Tanner chuckles but is cut off by Dawn calling me. I'm so close to landing the sponsorship deal, ready to officially launch my new team at the end of this upcoming tour. Just need to sign those goddamn papers.

"Ms. Rillerton ," I say as pleasantly as possible, even though someone else has just cut me off in traffic and blamed *me* for it. "I hope you're calling with some good news. Are those papers signed and on their way to me?"

She pauses for a little too long, and I grip the wheel tightly. "Look, Mr. Rhodes, I— I do apologize. Truly. Everything seemed to go fine, right up until we got the memo earlier yesterday morning."

"Memo?"

"It was sent through this morning from your company."

"I'm afraid I'm completely in the dark on this one, ma'am. It came from us? What did it say?"

She sighs heavily, warping the sound over the phone. "It was advising us on the update to the energy efficiency factor. As I'm sure you're aware, we're an environmentally conscious company, and having low emissions is important to us. We were already on the fence about sponsoring a racing team, but this rise is too much."

I count to five in my head. "I'm sorry to hear that; however, I can assure you that there have been no changes—"

"I apologize again. We won't be able to sign the sponsorship deal at this stage. We can't risk it. We're only a small company, and while we were looking to branch out into the States, it's just a touch too much for us at this time."

I manage a terse goodbye before she hangs up.

I know exactly who is behind that little stunt, and they're about to find out about it. *After* my appointment with Allyson Peters.

My mind is a mess of anger when I arrive at Elite Sports Physio, and I am furiously texting on my phone to Tanner, trying to work out the best course of action from here. We have three weeks of tour coming up with the intent to name the new team, complete with sponsorships, on the final race. It's been long enough.

We need to find a large-name sponsor and *fast*.

I'm so busy texting on my phone that I don't realize Allyson has walked into the waiting room.

I lift my gaze to meet hers, and our eyes lock, Allyson's widening in shock.

"Zander," she breathes.

There you are, gorgeous.

Chapter 2

Allyson

Seeing Zander Rhodes after almost fifteen years was not on my to-do list today. In fact, it's not on my to-do list *any* day. He got to choose to leave me when we were in college, he doesn't get to decide when to come back.

My stare hardens as his gaze greedily sweeps across my body, lingering below my eye line. "Mr. Rhodes," I say with a frown. "Long time no see. It was appreciated."

He lets out a smirk. God, time has done him well. Zander had been all skin and bone in college. Now he's thickened out to strong, gym-grown muscles and a sharp jawline. He's got tattoos that trace up his neck and a shaved head that makes him look far fiercer than he ever did in college. Zander still has that sweet look in his eyes, though. The tattoos, muscles, and lack of hair can't hide the tenderness that I'm well aware he possesses–when he wants to show it.

"What can I help you with?" I ask, glancing at my patient list, and... *damn*. It really does say 'Zander Rhodes' as my next patient. I throw a dirty look at Carmen, my receptionist, who never usually gives me the patient's details beforehand. I don't know why I assumed it would be different if it's *Zander Rhodes*. "I can't imagine it's PT-related." A sudden fear rushes through my head as I mentally calculate what my daughter is doing right now. She *should* be at school, but wasn't there something about a field trip? Was that today?

I frown at the form in front of me. "Oh." It is actually PT-related. "Well... I guess come on through. I'm sure one of my other therapists are available to—"

"You," he says. The first words out of his goddamn gorgeous mouth have been possessive. Sounds about right from memory. "I'm sure you can squeeze me into your schedule. You can't be that busy, seeing as my appointment was with you to begin with."

I square my shoulders and send him to my clinic room. I flash a glare at Carmen, who, behind Zander's back, is pretending to fan herself with our brochures.

"Fine," I say, following Zander into the room and sitting heavily at my computer. "Just take off your shirt while I load up my computer, and we can see what we're working with."

Zander smirks again but does as I requested. I firmly gaze at my computer screen while I put in his details. My eyes suddenly widen when I see the reason for his visit.

"Wait..." I turn to him as he struggles to control his grin. "Why the hell did you take your shirt off if it's for your leg?"

He laughs loudly, it bouncing off the walls. "You asked me to." He holds up his large hands. "You're the boss."

No ring, I see. Surprising. Maybe his college antics of finding whatever the next hottest thing was is still going on.

I turn back to the computer to get my mind off his abs. He certainly didn't have those in college.

"You need my pants off?" he says, and I can hear the wicked grin in his sentence.

"No. *No.*" I take a deep breath to get my bearings and spin to face him. "Right. First thing first, let me see you walk." I take a look at my notes. "It says here you were in a racing accident two years ago?"

"Mm."

I raise my eyebrow. "Still doing that, then?"

He still hasn't put his shirt back on and leans back, holding himself up on the bed, making all the waves of his body stretch and roll. It's something out of a wet dream.

I've had countless hot, muscular men come through my clinic doors, but none have affected me like Zander.

He gets off the bed and walks around the room, and I'm surprised I didn't notice it when he walked in. There's a slight twinge around the corners of his eyes that seems to come naturally the second he puts his left foot all the way down. I can usually tell when someone is dramatizing their pain when I'm watching, but Zander seems genuine.

"Okay, stand still?"

He stops, and his weight shifts to his right instinctively.

"Put as much pressure only on your left foot as you can and then hold it for as long as possible." I watch him do it and hum under my breath, turning back to my computer. All the previous therapist appointments have made it onto my system, and I whistle. "You've done this a lot."

"Too much," he mutters. "They all do the same thing. They give me exercises, some suggest surgery, some suggest stronger painkillers, but they all end up with saying I need to stop racing. I ain't quitting, sweetheart."

I narrow my eyes. "I'm not your sweetheart, Zander." I fold my arms and lean back in my chair. "So, what do you want me to do about it? You want me to tell you they're all wrong and you should keep racing?"

"You specialize in professional athletes. Thought you might know something they don't."

I study him and purse my lips. "I need to observe you. How you use your legs, the exercises you do, etcetera."

His gaze meets mine again, and there's that twinkle again. "Tonight, I'll be at the track. You can see exactly what I'm doing."

I match his energy. "I don't work out of hours," I say bluntly. "I will see you here next week for your next appointment. For the next week, can you please fill out this document so I can get an idea of your training schedule, exercise routines, and general use of your leg?"

He briefly regards me before clicking his tongue against the roof of his mouth, his gaze piercing onto mine. "Look, I don't have the time for that. I need this *thing*—" He gestures to his thigh. "—figured out before I waste any more time. I have other things to focus on, and my leg is just getting in the damn way. I need it fixed and fixed now."

"Yeah, you and the two WNBA players I have intensive rehab with, the ten-million-dollar linebacker who needs to be back on the field ASAP, and the professional snowboarder who has Olympic trials soon." I turn back to my computer. "A non-professional racecar driver is not a top priority, especially one that has been to fifteen other therapists in the last few years."

Zander puts his shirt back on and grins smugly. "The track tonight. I'll see you there." He quickly scrawls something on the back of his patient notes. His personal phone number and the address of the racetrack. "I'll be there from four."

He's gone before I can really object.

Just in time, too. My daughter shoulders her way into the clinic, staring down at her phone. She doesn't notice Zander, and he doesn't see her, and my heart restarts all over again.

I sink into the chair behind the desk as my best friend, Trina, who had been holding the door open for him to exit, finally enters, her eyes pinched with the hint of a memory.

"Was that...?"

I shoot her a look and glance at Hayley, her fourteen-year-old head still scrolling through her phone. Trina zips her lips shut and leans on the bench, turning to my daughter.

"Hayley, hon, I need your help again. What's that new dance move called? I need to put it on my socials."

Hayley rolls her eyes toward Trina and sits heavily in the plush armchairs I have in the waiting room. "Trina, we've talked about this. I'm not going to help you with dances anymore. They're not doing you any favors."

"Rude," Trina mutters before turning to me. "I've had three people quit my yoga classes in the last week. Three, Allyson."

"That's not so bad—"

"I only had nine!" I wince and try to busy myself with work, knowing what her next question will be. "Are you still sending people my way?"

"Oh... uh, yeah. Sometimes. If I feel the person is right for—"

Trina narrows her eyes, and even Hayley is looking at me with a smirk on her face. "So, you're not."

"I mean, I *am*. I just don't feel like we share the same type of people in our businesses, you know? You're a yoga studio in Los Angeles. You have to try something different to stand out."

Hayley grinned. "Yeah, you know this guy went viral recently because he started offering nude sex yoga classes."

Trina and I both look at Hayley with the same look of ill-disguised disgust. "Gross," Trina mutters.

I clasp Trina's hand and give a quick squeeze. "No need to resort to nude sex yoga, Trina, but find something you *can* do that will help you stand out."

Trina is one of those people who usually finds the positives in anything. Anything unrelated to her business, that is. Opening up her own yoga studio had been a dream for a long time, only realized when her OCD and dementia-struck mother passed away, and Trina was given a whole lot more free time. Whether the dream was fully realized before she opened the studio is another issue.

She groans loudly before turning to Hayley again because, apparently, a fourteen-year-old that spends more time online than in real life is the answer to all her problems. "Any suggestions?"

"Nah."

Trina throws me a dirty look before gesturing Hayley to the door. "Go to school, child. Get an education. Get away from that phone. I've learned it doesn't work anyway."

Hayley chuckles and glances at her before showing her phone screen. "I was actually looking up ways that you could be different for your studio, but *if you insist...*"

Trina's over there in a second, pulling up the chair next to her and scrolling through Hayley's phone with her.

"Both of you," I growl. "Out. Hayley, I'll probably be home late tonight. I have a... er, late meeting. Stay with Trina until I'm done."

"I think Rachel is having a sleepover. Can I go?"

"Rachel with the four older brothers or Rachel that lives with her creepy uncle?"

"Neither." She gives me a happy smile. "Rachel from down the street. You can call her mom if you like."

"*Oh.* Yeah. Of course. Tell her mom that the recipe for the salad saved my life last week."

Trina raises her eyebrows. "Bit dramatic."

Hayley nods, completely serious. "It's true. It was a family function at Grandma's. Nothing was edible apart from Mom's salad. It saved both of our lives."

Trina screws her nose up. "I won't ask any more follow-up questions."

Hayley gets up and nods towards the door. "Let's go next door to your studio and see what we can do." They both wave a quick goodbye before they trail out of the building. "Right, so do you want to go viral like nude sex yoga guy? Or do you want to be, like, *relevant*?"

"Let's just shelve the nude sex yoga for now, okay? I don't think I'll be able to find the right permits."

I chuckle as the door swings shut behind them before looking down at Zander's patient form in my hand.

Four p.m. Griffin Motorsports. See you there, sweetheart.

I sigh and hope like hell to get out of all this unscathed, unlike last time.

Did you enjoy this sneak peek?

Scan this QR Code to visit the Amazon Kindle store page for
Damaged Bad Boy Billionaire

Thank You

Thank you for reading ***Damaged Billionaire's Surprise Heir***.

Reviews allow others to learn about my books (and keep me writing) so I would appreciate it if you could drop me an honest review on Amazon.

The QR code below will take you to this book's Amazon page.

It only takes a few seconds, and this is easiest way you can support my continued writing efforts.

If you are a romance bookworm and would like to receive an advance reader copy (ARC) of my future books, do sign up to join my ARC team at **gwynne.vip/arc**

"No entertainment is so cheap as reading, nor any pleasure so lasting."
—Mary Wortley Montagu

Printed in Great Britain
by Amazon

40649182R10128